The Ascent of Love

Rooprashi

Invincible Publishers

First published in India in 2019

ISBN : 978-93-88333-67-2

Invincible Publishers

Registered Address: 201A, SAS Tower, Sector 38,
Gurgaon-122003

Printed at Thomson Press (India) LTD

Lipi Gupta

Freelance Editor, Writer, Blogger
(Gully Writers) and Psychologist.

Dedicated To

My Beloved Baauji

Love surpasses every other feeling. It is love that keeps us bonded to our loved ones, even after death. This book is dedicated to my handsome Daadaji **Late Shri Vidya Dhar Sharma** (Baauji).

He was mostly engrossed in his books since I can remember. He has been my biggest inspiration and the reason of my love for books.

When my 90 years old Baauji read my debut book "The Girl Who Saw It All", I experienced the amazing feeling of what it is like to make my grandparent proud. Those eyes had aged, but I could clearly see the pride in them, as if I had fulfilled his dream of writing a book.

Baauji, I know you must be having an amazing time wherever you are, just like you lived your life, on your own terms and inspired everyone around you. My love for you will keep growing as you are an indispensable part of my personality. I pray to God that I be given another chance to meet you in this world or the other. Thank you for being my Baauji. I Miss You.

Acknowledgements

"When are you going to write your next book?"

"I have no idea. I do not know if I will write any more books."

"You will."

I am so blessed to have these people around me who harboured the confidence that I was going to write this book. They are the ones who repeatedly kept asking me the question until I knew what I was going to write about in my next book. I am indebted to them and their selfless love.

The first person on the list is the very talented photographer and sketch artist, **Ms. Anukampa Sharma** (email: anukampa1989@gmail.com; Instagram @astralrover_). I thank you for being an inspiration and sharing your views at every stage of writing this book. Most importantly, I am thankful that you took out time from your busy schedule and designed the beautiful sketches for the book. You are such a beautiful soul and a talented creative person with such out-of-the-box thinking.

My sweetheart friend and editor of this book, **Ms. Lipi Gupta** (lipigupta04@gmail.com). I am so thankful for all her efforts and for giving me her honest opinions at every stage of writing the book. She is so brutally honest in her opinions that sometimes I want her to lie a bit about some things, but thankfully she did not and did her best with the editing of the script.

My website designer **Mr. Vikash Singh** (www.finesofttechnologies.com). He is a true gentleman and very professional in his work. His team is right there whenever I have faced any website related issue. They are so prompt in their response and resolving issues. Thank you for being such a strong support.

My family, specially my baby daughter, **Shanaya**, for asking me questions all the time and making me see things from a different perspective.

Lastly, but most importantly, my heartfelt thanks to my readers who want me to write more. You are the ones who spend your time reading my books and giving my writing good worth. Keep sharing your reviews. Readers' reviews are an author's tonic.

"And It Sings To My Heart, Like A Melody Carved From My Unexplored Profoundness.

Creating Rhythm In My Unequal Breaths And A Dance Completing My Soul."

Anukampa Sharma (@astralrover_)
Freelance Sketch Artist & Photographer

One

'What a mess?' The thought crossed my mind as I saw the mess strewn across the room. The master bedroom of our house has been more familiar to me rather than the rest because it had been officially mine since always. Today, it was in the worst condition. From toiletries to clothes, everything was scattered all over the bed and the floor, while I was trying to choose which ones to be packed and which ones to be left at home.

To be honest, the condition of this room usually was messy or mostly messy. But today, it had crossed all limits. There was no space left to move on the floor and everything was scattered where the floor should have been.

By the way did I just say? 'The Master Bedroom?' Why do we call it a Master Bedroom? Seems like a gender bias here too, doesn't it? Okay I guess my thoughts can win long jump medals in the Olympics, given that they can really make long leaps without once touching the hard ground. 'But why is this room called a master bedroom when it has belonged to a Miss? Can't it be called Madam Bedroom or any other female name?'

At this moment, when I should be thinking about which clothes should be packed to be taken along and about the train that I had to catch early morning, my thoughts were drifting to all the feminism and gender bias issues that I had been experiencing all my life. But to be true, packing is sometimes the most difficult task, especially when you are really very excited for a trip and least bothered about the clothes. Mostly, I ended up packing extra luggage, even though I was determined not to do it this time. But now that I had taken out most of the clothes from my cupboard, I was very confused which ones should accompany me on this journey.

"How are you going to survive in such cold weather of Kashmir with only one sweater?", Mom asked me, concerned, as she saw me taking out the only sweater I had packed in my bag.

"Mom, it's not that cold. January is almost over and I am going to get everything from jacket to the quilt at the institute itself. I will wear one warm jacket when I'll be leaving from here and I am sure it will be enough for this cold. I need to trek the mountains and it will be good if I carry minimum luggage."

"Still. I think you should carry at least one more sweater. You can never know in advance about any weather changes." Mom was trying so hard to convince me.

"My sweet mommy, why do you worry so much about me? I am grown up now. I can take care of myself". I hugged my mom lovingly. I think I was already missing her. Being away from her was still the one of the toughest things for me and it feels just like the first day of my hostel.

Hi, I am Taara Singh. Now, if you are wondering 'what kind of name is this?', I want to tell you that you are not alone. I hated my name from the time I had gained enough sense to have an opinion. I found my name masculine and pretty weird. I still do not understand why parents actually choose such names for their babies. Babies are so small. They cannot even protest it. Till the time comes that the kid is grown enough to protest, until that time all the documents, including date of birth certificate, have this weird name stuck across and it becomes permanent. So you see, I had to accept that I have to be Taara Singh for the rest of my life. I had compromised with this fact long ago. But I guess my stars had plotted something else in their pattern. I was finally able to accept my name, but soon after, this movie called 'Gadar' was released to add to my misery. Yes, because it was not Ameesha Patel, but Sunny Deol who was named Taara Singh in it and it is understandable because it is a masculine name. Now, my friends teased me with its dialogues and songs every chance they got.

"Don't irritate her, you know, or else Taara Singh will un-root the hand pump and will throw it at us."

Whenever I parked my scooty someone around me would be singing, "Main nikla gaddi leke..." I had to forcibly smile at these irritating jokes on me to appear polite. I never understood the reason as to why I could not ever tell them that I hated these jokes, just like my name.

By the way, I am an engineer in a multinational company in Noida. I live with my loving (except the naming incident) family in New Delhi. I did my engineering from Dehradun. But more than being an engineer, I am actually a sportsperson at heart. I love to trek mountains. It's fun, relaxing and really thrilling. But as much as I'd have loved to do this a long time ago, this is the first time I am going for a formal training in mountaineering and it's going to be more challenging this time. But I love to challenge myself. I love to see myself grow. Mountains are slowly becoming my passion and I am getting intoxicated by them. Just like an obsessed lover, I am deeply in love with them.

I have gone to many mountainous expeditions in Himachal Pradesh and West Bengal. But this time, it is Kashmir. Kashmir is a beautiful experience for all Indian mountaineers. Every new experience in the mountains has brought me closer to my life and most importantly to my own self. I love to be away from the busy world, where everyone is rushing to achieve earthly goals. Mountains bring me peace of mind and I feel that my life becomes more purposeful when I am closer to nature. Sometimes, I feel I was born in the wrong time. I love everything real and natural, while here everything feels artificial and fake. When I see others who are living happily in this world of fake smiles and holding grudges deep inside, I often wonder if I am the only odd one out who has felt this way. or others too did and have somehow grown out of it and forgot it behind their fake smiles. May be they have become habitual of this life and pretending to be happy seems real to them.

The world where emotions have become emojis and cheese has become tofu, the superficial expression of feelings suffocates me sometimes. That is when I pack my bags and leave to be with my beloved mountains.

Two

"Taara, have you thought about the marriage proposal that I told you about a few days back. You said you will think about it. So, did you?" Mom was collecting the clothes lying on the floor but I knew her eyes were fixed on my expressions. She sounded hopeful to get some positive reply after the small discussion about life we had the other day. But she kept picking up and folding the clothes that I had rejected.

"Hmm… No mom… I did not." I don't know why I was not even able to think of getting married. Actually, to be true, I think I do not even need a husband. In fact, if necessary, I need a mom like husband who will take care of me like she does; who will take care of me like this after my marriage? Everyone will expect me to take care of them. Marriage is a bad idea right now. I will be at a loss. So not me. I am still trying to find a reason why I do not want to get married. But I knew I did not want to.

"Taara beta, you cannot live your life alone. You will need someone to spend your life with. We are here with you today, tomorrow even. But we won't be here forever".

"Mom, don't be so emotional. I understand what you are saying. But I won't get married till I feel like getting married. I won't marry because of society or the age factor."

"But, beta, the reality is that you will not find a good match after a certain age."

"Okay, mom. I will think about it, but, after this trip. Right now, I am too excited for this trip".

"Huhhh.... It's already late now. I think the packing is almost done. You should sleep now. Else, you will miss the train in the morning. Good night beta". Mom walked out of the room, switching off the light as she left. Her efforts to convince me for the marriage had failed yet again.

"Mom, I Love You".

"Love you too, beta. Go to sleep now". Mom had her usual cute smile on her face and went out of the room.

'How do mothers work so hard the whole day and still manage to smile, even when they are too tired to. I can never be like this. Why does everyone have to get married? Maybe I am unmarriageable. Am I unmarriageable?' Now though I wasn't ready to get married, that was still an unnerving thought.

'Unmarriageable? What does that word mean? Does it even have a meaning? Maybe I have invented a new word today or is it already there? Whatever is the case, I think it should mean that marriage is not meant for me'. I smiled at my own thoughts.

I had always been amazed at the feeling of going to mountains and trips with a new group every time. The trips with strangers brought freshness in itself. I got a chance to know different people, understand human nature better, be in different cultures, overcome my insecurities and dig deeper into myself. I was quite excited about this mountaineering course.

'Even a lifetime is not enough to understand yourself then how can we expect to understand others too in the same lifetime. Maybe this is what soul mates are meant to be. Maybe they are called soul mates because they understand each other easily. Am I yet to meet my soul mate? Or maybe I had already found mine and lost him? Was it the right decision?' Smiling at my thoughts weren't the only expressions I had. I had these disturbing thoughts and at such time, it was important that I tried sleeping even more earnestly.

But sleep is one the few things that doesn't come with effort. Rather, it runs away. At the end of the day, when our mind is at peace and we are in our bed, it is the time when we listen to our heart loud and clear. The heart tries to convey its views to us most of the time but we ignore them because of our busy schedules in day. But at night, those thoughts come back again and they hover around in our mind. This was one of those nights when the thoughts wouldn't stop hovering.

Three

It is twenty sixth of January today, the date I had met him five years back. It was our anniversary again and the day was almost over now.

"I still miss you Vedant".

Whenever I thought about our first meeting, I thought about his eyes. Somehow, those eyes flashed like a highlighted memory every time I even think of that moment. No one ever saw me with so much love as those two eyes did. I tried to forget those eyes after we broke up, but I always failed.

I had thought that this wound would heal over time but I was wrong. I still loved him. Maybe it was this unfulfilled desire that I still hoped to fulfil or a feeling that I may never be able to. It made me feel like I had already met my soul mate in this life and somehow lost my chance to be with him.

The bond I felt with Vedant could not be explained in words, but it was a connection that was still important to me; a connection which was pure, directly linked to my soul. Why I am not able to forget him even after all these years? God knows the answer to that. He would be married by now. He would probably be a dad even. We are not even in touch since our breakup. But then, what is still holding me to his memories? I had not been able to figure that out. May be I know him from one of my many previous births; maybe even more. But then why did I go away from him? Why did I break his heart? Could I not be happy with him? Could I have been happy with him and not seen it?

I am still so amazed how this one person had touched my heart, my soul and changed my life forever. People say that these wounds heal with time.

'But it has been five years now. Why do I still remember you? Why do I still try to find you whenever I go to the mountains? Do you even think of me once? Have you moved on? How do I move on? Tell me Vedant, how do I move on? I broke myself by going away from you but never understood how to heal myself. What should I do to relieve my heart from this pain?' The words were pouring out of my mouth like the tears were pouring out of my eyes.

This was not the first time that I was weeping before sleeping, never knowing when my thoughts turned into dreams. It had happened many times in these years. Fighting with my own thoughts and trying to find the answers, I did not realize when I dozed off to sleep.

It seemed like a festival. A crowd. People were enjoying themselves and that made it seem like a celebration was going on. Adults were busy shopping and kids were having fun on different types of rides that were exciting enough to make the kids go crazy wanting to ride them again and again. Everyone was happy and in a festive mode. I was enjoying my favourite ride, the Columbus. I had always preferred to be among the kids and usually found their chats more lively and interesting. Their feelings filled with innocence, curiosity and the enthusiasm of being able to understand small things that we adult have forgotten to enjoy. I loved the feeling when the ride was coming down from such a height. To be honest, I felt like a kid myself. The sense of adrenaline rush made this ride even more exciting. Suddenly, my eyes wandered to a man in the crowd and remained stuck on him. Though it was his back that was towards me, I felt I knew that it was him. It felt so sudden that it made me apprehensive. Suddenly, I wanted the ride to stop immediately. A strange feeling arose in me as if I was looking at my soul mate, the one my soul craved to find. He started walking and was going in the other direction. I felt a desperation that I cannot do anything but see him go away. Every nerve in my body was willing me to stop him, but no matter what, he was still walking in the other direction.

As soon as the ride stopped, I got off hurriedly and went in the direction where I had seen him. I wanted to stop him. I wanted to talk to him, to tell him how much I had waited for him. It felt strange that I hadn't actually seen the face or anything but I wanted to be with him till eternity.

I could still see him going away and I did nothing. I tried running to that spot but he had started way before I could reach him. I tried to follow him behind people but just as suddenly as it happened, he was lost in the crowd.

'TRINNNNNNNNNNNNNNNN...' The morning alarm rang loudly in my dreams as my sleep tried to linger on, just to save the dream from fading away. But like all things, it receded deep into my brain and I woke up from the weird dream.

I sighed as I got back to the real world. 'I need to catch my train in sometime. I should get ready'. The thought was in the forefront of my brain, but so was my dream. It was refusing to fade away even with my eyes closed.

'The man in my dream… was it Vedant? How did I have such a weird dream? It must be Vedant. I was thinking of him last night. Or maybe, I am going to find my soul mate on this trip. Maybe this dream was an indication of that.' The desperation was still lingering in my heart but a smile crossed my face as the thought forced my eyes to open wide. I smiled to myself and got off the bed happily. Maybe it was an indication of me meeting someone important in my life;

or, just the fact that I was ready to move on. But it felt good somehow. It wasn't a sad dream. It was a happy dream.

Four

"Oho, are you taking only this much luggage?" Younger brothers tease their sisters no matter what. Pranay wasn't an exception. If the luggage would have been bigger, he would have teased me the other way around.

However, I was in no mood to get into a conversation. I hated getting up early in the morning and I hated talking for at least an hour after waking up. It was a heavy task to do. Pranay was just totally opposite of me. He could talk non-stop just after waking up and left no chance to tease and irritate me, even this early in the morning.

But today, I didn't feel like arguing with him. Today, I felt like ignoring his comment and so I smiled at him. I knew I was going to be away from home for the coming days and I was definitely going to miss my stupid, but cute, brother. I guess he felt the same way because his teasing smile was warmer than usual.

"I do not understand how you will carry so many items of luggage with you". Okay, I got it wrong. I thought he was saying my luggage was less. He, on the other hand, did not stop talking.

"I will carry them. Do not worry. Just brush your teeth and get ready fast. You need to carry this luggage at railway station to drop me to the train. You are the only coolie we have in our house". I replied and started laughing. I had tried my best to stop this brother-sister world war, but seriously I could not control myself finally. After all, I wouldn't get to fight with him for a long time after today.

"I am not a coolie and I am not going to carry your luggage. I am not going with you. Mom, she called me Coolie." His pitch was high and I felt elated having pissed him off.

"Haha. You are a coolie and if you won't brush your teeth, you are not going to get customers too. People will run away from you because of your deadly bad breath. How will you earn then...huh?" I teased him again. It felt good arguing with him. Plus, I knew mom would not take his side today. I was leaving.

"Okay, I am going to brush my teeth and I will go with you to railway station. But mind you, I won't carry your luggage because I am not a coolie". He announced every word with extra stress on the vowels and ran to the bathroom.

"Okay". I laughed seeing him surrender. Generally, I have to surrender to him. He must be feeling bad that I am going.

"Pranay, stop fighting with your sister and get ready fast. We are getting late. Taara should not miss her train". Dad's announcement came too little too late as he entered the room.

"Everyone scolds me in this house. It's always my mistake. No one says anything to Taara. She is after all Papa's 'Pari' and what am I? I am the devil of this house". Pranay's muffled and irritated voice was coming out of the bathroom. Dad and I suddenly felt like laughing loudly. Poor Pranay!

"So is everything ready Taara?"

"Yes Dad"

"Do you need anything else?" I shook my head so he continued. "All the best beta. Do take care of yourself. It is a risky course. Do whatever your trainers say".

"Yes Dad. I will. Thanks Dad."

Soon, it was time to leave for the railway station. I hugged my mom. Her eyes were red. She knew I was just going for a few days. But she felt like crying no matter what. Dad and Pranay prepared to drop me at the railway station.

The station was over-crowded, like always. Pranay and I hurriedly headed towards the platform where their train was expected to arrive. No matter how early you get to the platform, it always feels like you must run so you don't miss the train. It felt like one of the opportunities in life which we need to grab at the right time.

I was running with the bag in my hand trying to make room in the fast moving crowd around, when someone's foot got entangled in mine. The ground beneath me suddenly felt like it had been swept away as I fell down on the platform.

Pranay stopped and looked back when he could not see me around. I was thinking of calling him for help, when he saw me on the ground and came running.

"Are you okay?" He gave me his hand to get up and thank God that he didn't try to click a picture of mine like I had done last month when he slipped on water. I still have the funny picture though I lied to him that I deleted it

"Yes, I am fine". I lied while covering up my hurt foot and back.

"Thank God. Have all the people in the world arrived at the New Delhi Railway Station? I do not have to run too, you know. I was just standing and it seemed to me as if the crowd was carrying me along with it." Pranay was a typical Delhite in some ways.

We had reached the platform and both of us were almost out of breath after running so fast. We saw people around us were also trying to catch their breath. Maybe everyone comes late to the platforms.

"It's good that dad stayed in the car at the parking. He would not be able to walk this fast to catch your train". Pranay was looking in either directions of the platform. "I think your train will be arriving any moment".

"Can you check the status of my train, Pranay?"

"The train is on time. I have already checked". He smiled.

"Okay".

"Mom was worried about your food. Have it on time and beware of the strangers in the train. Try to be more vigilant. Don't stray on the platforms. The train won't stop for too long." Pranay sounded like an elder brother. Maybe he was growing up.

"Okay, grandpa". I laughed but I felt proud of him. I looked at him lovingly. I knew he was going to miss me too and loved it when Pranay showed care. But then, he showed me his tongue.

"No no. I am not saying this. Do not think that I care for you. This is what mom and dad asked me to tell you". He said instantly covering up.

"Haha. Okay, okay. I will not think that way. Happy now?"

The train was arriving. We got ready with the luggage and started walking towards the coach.

"I will miss you, bhai". My eyes felt heavier as the tears threatened to roll out.

"I will try to miss you too and do not walk too fast on the mountains. Fat people can roll down if they walk fast."

Pranay was laughing and teased me of the fall that I just had some time back.

Maybe I won't miss him as much. Who am I kidding? I knew I would. "Okay, I will keep this in mind". I was laughing too. I'd not get this fun time with him for some time now.

"You take care of yourself, mom and dad". I hugged him and kissed him on his cheek. Then, I climbed on the coach.

The train had started to move slowly. We waved at each other till the time we couldn't see each other anymore. The train had started to gain speed and soon, the running city of Delhi started running in the opposite direction from me.

Five

Vedant

I was sitting by my hostel room window, with tears in my eyes and a strange heaviness in my heart. I could still see my mother who was walking far away from me, at the hostel gate completing the formalities.

"Please take care of my daughter. She was admitted here today only. Do get her things that she wants from outside". She was telling the hostel guard who was the only medium for girls in the hostel to get things they needed from outside. I couldn't actually hear her. But the voice was clear in my head. She was always worried about me.

The rules were very strict here. Going outside was allowed only with the Warden's permission, so mostly girls requested the guard to get things from outside. I wanted to run down the hostel stairs and hug my mother. I wanted to tell her that I loved her and did not want to be away from her. Sometimes we feel this sudden urge to express our love, but the situation does not allow us to do so. While when we are mostly with the people we love, we tend to ignore the things like expression of love, being thankful for being there. I badly wanted to be with my mother that very moment and tell her how much I loved her.

I had thought about this day many times during my school days and had felt excited about it. But I had never imagined that this was going to be so painful, emotionally. I had never felt like this before. This was a strange feeling of living away from your mother especially when she is your friend too.

'Mom had told me how much I cried while going to school when I was a kid. How I used to embrace her and did not let her go. I feel the same way even today. I didn't want to let her go even today. It's just that I had grown up now and had learnt to control my feelings. I had become habitual of suppressing the real emotions. But I still wanted to embrace her tight and tell her not to leave me alone'.

"Please don't go". The words escaped my mouth as the thought of being away from her was stuck in my head and tears rolled down my cheeks. "People say hostel life is fun. But all I want right now is to get away from here. How would I live without mom? I am already missing her so much".

Though Dad has always been a bit strict but I believed I could never live without him either. My tears grew heavier as they had now turned into full-fledged sobbing.

We learn to hide our emotions and suppress them to behave as per the societal norms. But this does not change the real us. Deep within, we are still the same person who feels the same way.

I dragged my hostel bed and slid it to the window. I wanted to sit near the window side and look outside. Right now, this seemed like the only option that would bring peace to me. My mom had long gone, out of the hostel gate. I was feeling so homesick, so soon. I kept looking outside and did not realize when I fell asleep. I had no idea that the coming days were going to change my life forever.

I stepped into the main gate of my college campus in Dehradun. I had mixed feelings of excitement and nervousness. The excitement was about the beginning of a new phase in life; the college life which I had heard was going to be the best days of my life.

As I entered the college gate, it opened my way to a new life and it was nothing less than what I had imagined my college would be like. I walked through the college entrance and had first glimpse of the place where I was going to spend the next four years of my life. Engineering was going to be a new adventure for me. As I walked through the long corridor, trying to figure out which classroom I had to go to, I saw a group of students calling me. I went towards them. I had heard about the ragging in the college.

'Are they calling me to rag me?' The thought passed my mind as I walked towards them.

"Are you a new admission?" The voice belonged to a girl with black hair and a smooth face. She had that senior batch attitude in her way of talking.

"Yes".

"You should say 'Yes Ma'am' then. We all are your seniors. Remember to say 'Sir' or 'Ma'am' while talking to any of us". She said arrogantly.

I felt a little embarrassed for the way she spoke but refrained from talking too much. "Okay, Ma'am".

"What is your name?"

"Taara"

"Taara, what?"

"Taara Singh"

"Oh, Taara...Singh. The one in the movie Gadar?" She laughed loudly and the whole group followed suite.

'Oh yeah, I am the same Taara Singh and this is such a new joke,' I wanted to say but kept mum.

"Which course have you taken admission in?" She still was not over with me.

"Mechanical engineering"

"Oh, mechanical," she said, rotating her eyeballs three sixty degrees. Suddenly, she started laughing in a high pitched voice making fun of me and the group followed the laugh.

"What made you get into this field?" Another girl from the group asked, trying to control her laughter.

"Ma'am, I like this field and thought I will do good in it". I could not understand the reason for their laughter.

"You like this field? You like mechanical or you did not get admission in any other field?" One more girl joined the mocking conversation and the group laughed harder.

I was listening to them, not knowing what to say. I had an apt reply to shut their mouths but I was trying to avoid any conflict on the very first day of the college.

"Ma'am, I know not many girls prefer mechanical engineering. This field is mostly chosen by boys. But I really wanted to get into this stream. I have never been bothered by others perceptions. I do what I feel like doing". I surprised myself at my sudden display of confidence.

"Hey, let's make her dance on that song from movie Gadar. Main Nikla Gaddi Leke." That was another weird girl in the group and everyone got excited at her out-of-the-box suggestion.

"What? Shit. Shut up weirdo". That's what I wanted to say. I so didn't want to dance on the song. Weren't the other jokes enough?

"Hey, Dean Sir is coming this way. It's our class time. Let's go," a girl from the group looked at the opposite direction and reported, interrupting my thoughts. They all ran towards their class as if a cop was coming to catch a thief. Whenever it comes to bullies, they are cowards at heart, hunting in packs and scared of authorities.

'Thank god they are gone'. My heart was seriously happy that I didn't have to fight or become a joker on my first day of college. The college guard was near to the entrance gate and I decided to ask about the direction of my classroom so I don't run into more bullies.

"Hey… Hi". I heard a guy's voice.

I turned and saw a very familiar guy coming towards me. By chance, I looked straight in his eyes and even they seemed familiar. I had definitely seen him somewhere. 'Oh yes, he is the same guy I had met while filling my admission form in the college. But we did not talk at that time'. Well, I guess now we will.

He was looking at me with his innocent puppy eyes, smiling. I could not help but smile back. I observed his tall, muscular physique as he wore a tight t-shirt. It seemed like he visited the gym and is one of those Salman Khan fans. Okay, my mind was having random, quick thoughts.

"Hi. I am Vedant. I am a student of third year Mechanical Engineering. We met at the admissions office that day. Remember?"

"Yeah, I do"

"Actually, I overheard your conversation with that group of girls and really liked the way you replied".

"Thanks. As long as they don't want to bully me again". At least someone paid attention to my reply. He doesn't look like a guy who is hiding in shadows, scared of bullies.

"I think your class will be in classroom number four on the first floor. Freshers have most of their classes there. Near the HOD's office".

"Thank you".

"Have a nice day". He smiled and waved good-bye.

"You too". I smiled and waved back.

Six

Kashmir

The train service was till Udhampur. I reached late in the evening and stayed at my Maasi's place. Udhampur had a beautiful station, with scenic beauty.

'Thank God I have relatives throughout India. Many things become a lot more comfortable'. I was feeling thankful to my mom's sister for her decision to get married here. Udhampur is a beautiful town in Jammu and Kashmir. I was already in love with its railway station. It was small, simple and surrounded by mountains. The feeling of being near the mountains was creeping over me and I loved it. It felt like I had started taking my first steps towards them and that filled me with a certain sense of relief and excitement at the same time.

I caught a shared taxi to Kashmir early morning the next day, as per the plan. The road ahead was good till some distance, but after a little while, the road became less broad and broken. It was not a smooth drive; it never is in the mountains. But the view outside was good enough for us passengers to deviate our thoughts from the road to the natural beauty around us.

The mountains had fewer plantations. In some areas, the plantation was very less and more of the soil on the mountains

was visible. As if some construction was going on there. But as we crossed the Jawahar tunnel, the view totally changed. We suddenly had beautiful lush green mountains around us. A valley surrounded by mesmerizing mountains and open fields whose beauty cannot be expressed in words.

"Oh my God. It's so beautiful. It seems like we have entered a new world. So purely beautiful… and so beautifully pure". A fellow passenger was exclaiming, every five minutes.

The mountains suddenly changed and became so very green. It seemed like a magic trick. The world was so different on both the ends of the Jawahar Tunnel.

'Maybe this is the reason why we call Kashmir as heaven on earth. Its breath-taking beauty is not comparable to any place on earth'. The thoughts were racing through my mind but my breath was slow and composed. Like always, and surprisingly every time, it felt like I was home.

Earlier the mountains which had seemed so far had suddenly come closer. I could see the starting point of the mountain as well as its tip. I wanted to climb them all at the same time. I was falling so much in love with this place. There were some mountains on which the stone seemed reddish in colour. They were adding to the beauty. As I had a closer look, I could see many plants had grown through the cracks in the stones. The taxi route was so that we were repeatedly going towards and away from the mountain. Everything that I could see made me long to touch the mountains more and more.

'Even plants grow and make spaces from cracks. Then why cannot we humans make space for ourselves? Why do we hesitate in doing what we really want to do? What stops us? What resistance do we have?'

"Madam, do you want to eat some apples? Special Apples from Kashmir". A boy about ten years old brought me back from my reverie. He had come to sell apples as our car had stopped at a traffic signal for some time. It was a wonder that so many people were here too. Like they too knew what a beautiful place it is that they decided to visit it like me.

"Yes. I will buy a few". I had heard a lot about the apples in Kashmir. They were considered juicier and tastier than the normal apples.

I bought some apples from him. They were different, very small in size and very tasty. Whatever people say about the Kashmir apple is so true. They taste really good. I could eat one complete apple in two or three bites and kept on wanting more. I ate all that I had bought. It may be the effect of the hunger and also the apples' tasted so nice that I felt like eating more and more. It's been some time since I had my breakfast so early in the morning. So naturally, I was very hungry too. But taste of the apples had their fair share of awe that made me have them all in one go.

'This is just the beginning. I wish this trip to be an adventurous one. I know the trip will be very adventurous'. My thoughts were as fresh as the air and that filled me with enthusiasm. I plugged in my earphones. I wanted to enjoy this moment with my favourite music and kept on looking at the beauty around us.

The shared taxi dropped me at Lal Chowk from where I took another taxi to the Mountaineering institute. This one was not shared.

"Madam ji, you will have to pay one thousand rupees to go to this area of Kashmir". The taxi driver informed me and felt reluctant to bargain.

I thought of bargaining but then, I left the idea. May be because of my pleasant mood at this beautiful place, I was not in a mood to argue about the rates however it was usually very hard for me to resist bargaining. Proper Delhite behaviour, I guess.

I took the taxi and wanted to enjoy my journey to the institute. I was looking around the place with a lot of curiosity. I was still at Lal Chowk.

'This is the place which is mostly in the news because of the terrorism. It seems so peaceful right now. How could this be so violent? How could such a beautiful place be soaked in blood?' I wondered.

There was a strange feeling that I was going through. A feeling of pain mixed with patriotism. A feeling of feeling unsafe in one's own country, mixed with love for your nation;... a feeling of helplessness to control such bloodshed and inhumanity but knowing that alone I can't. We all need to do that together.

"YE DIL NA HOTA BECHARA..." The taxi driver's booming voice brought me back from my thoughts. He had turned up the volume of the song and was singing along. He had a beautiful voice and was enjoying the song. His voice felt happy like he felt nothing that I felt about this place. When he finished the song, he looked calm.

"Bhaiya you sing so well. You love singing, don't you?"

"Madam ji, I love to sing. But I like old songs. Old songs are evergreen, full of emotions and good music. The modern music is more of noise". I nodded with a laugh. "Madam ji, the music is my life here. This helps us survive boredom here. When tourists come, I listen to music in my taxi. Else, when we have bad days and no tourists come here, we have to sit at home, play cards with friends and listen to music. The whole day we have nothing to do. But music is there and it is my life". He said with a tinge of sarcasm as well as sadness in his voice.

"I wanted to be a singer. But life had other plans. So, I try to fulfil my dream this way. I sing when I drive". He told me after a short pause. "What can we do? It is my destiny."

I did not say anything but was wondering about the unpredictability of life which we call destiny. He wanted to be a singer but could not become one. Didn't he try much or he didn't try at all? Do we get everything we try to achieve? Didn't I try enough? Maybe some things weren't just meant to be.

The thoughts in my mind were running parallel to the beautiful scenic views and I wanted to fly higher and higher. We all have wings but we need to realize our potential because there are no limits to flying higher and higher. The lion is the king of the jungle because it has this realization and knows it's potential.

“Bhaiya, where can I have something to eat? I am very hungry”. The mountains and the whirlpool of my thoughts were making me feel the hunger even more. Maybe I wasn’t exercising but my mind was doing that for my body.

“Madam ji, there is a small restaurant of my relative on the way. Would you like to go there?” He was hopeful and looked innocent.

“Yes, sure”. I was really hungry again. It felt like I had not eaten anything at all, which wasn’t true.

After fifteen minutes, we were at the Kashmir-e-shan Dhaba which was a small but clean place. The eating choices were less. So, I ordered Kasmiri Dum Aloo and rice as it was the only thing available at those late lunch hours.

After placing the order, I went out to look around the place. The Dhaba was on the road side and had a beautiful view of the valley in front. I sat on a big stone outside the dhaba and was having a view of the valley when I realized the pain in my back and ankle. I realized I had been hurt badly in that fall at the railway station. If this pain worsens, I will be unable to complete this training. I didn’t even pack a pain ointment. So I decided to get up to do some muscle stretching to relieve the pain. Soon, I saw the dhaba waala asking me to come back inside to have the food as the food was ready.

I went inside, grabbed a chair near the table and had my food. It felt pretty homely, like a mother had cooked it instead of a dhaba waala. ‘The hospitality of people in this restaurant and the yummy food they served cannot be compared to even a five star hotel. I am never going to forget this taste in my entire life’. I felt thankful to the taxi waala as I saw him waiting for me in the taxi.

“Did you eat?”

“Yes. He is my brother. My aunt cooks in the dhaba. Did you like the food, madamji?”

“Yes. Very tasty.”

I had relished the local Kashmiri food, breathed in the beauty of Kashmir and stretched my legs. All that was left was to reach the mountaineering institute. So, we started out on the rest of the journey.

Seven

MOUNTAINEERING INSTITUTE

Standing at the gate of the institute, I was wondering how to carry the luggage inside. The gate-keeper was not allowing any vehicle to go inside. The institute was still at least at a walking distance of three kilometres from the gate.

"Please allow my taxi to go inside. How will I carry this luggage such a long distance?" I requested the security guard at the gate.

"Ma'am, you are a mountaineer. You have come here to climb heights. Such questions are not expected from the mountaineers here". He said in a bit of a sarcastic tone.

His words stirred something inside me. He was actually right. How can I expect to complete this course if I am not confident enough to walk even this much of a distance? He had unknowingly motivated me with his sarcasm and had reminded me of my purpose of coming all the way to Kashmir.

I paid the taxi fare to the driver. I did not have a rucksack but a heavy traveller's bag and the thought of carrying the luggage bag in hand wasn't good for my aching ankles. I was looking at my bag trying to will it to become a rucksack when an idea struck me. I made a rucksack from the normal bag by putting my arms across the two hand grips and carried it on my back. The gatekeeper's words had injected a new spree in me. I wanted to walk the path to my destination with full zeal.

I was still feeling the pain in my back and ankle. But the happiness of being at the institute overpowered the feeling of pain. A small zoo was there on both sides of the road as I started walking. I was looking at the zoo and saw the animals that were roaming around. I saw a deer at first and then the bears. After the animal's section, there was a section for beautiful birds which were in so many colours and sizes. However, I didn't know much about their species, but I felt all of them were beautiful in their own way.

The walls around the institute were covered with different kinds of hanging plants. The trees covered all the area around and everything seemed so beautiful and serene.

I had walked, what I felt was long enough to be twenty kilometres, when I finally saw the statue of Tenzing Norgay, one of the first ones to climb Mount Everest. I was pretty tired to recognize him in the statue and had to read the name on the placard underneath, which said 'Brave Man, Tenzing Norgay'.

'He was indeed a brave man and deserved the honour,' I thought as I passed his statue and moved on towards the institute building.

I saw a queue outside the reception room and many bags were lying there. The queue was for the booking confirmation for the mountaineering course. I too waited in the queue and noticed a girl standing in the row, shuffling her legs. The girl in the row was tall enough for everyone to notice her. More importantly, she was blocking the view in the queue due to her height. Everyone was expectantly looking around and so was I, till, finally my turn came.

My booking was confirmed and I was informed about my room number. I felt like a huge elephant had moved ahead which I hadn't realized was there, till now. Finally, I felt, everything was happening. I was allotted the room number five in the hostel. After this, soon, I was handed over my stuff that was important for survival in the hostel. The stuff comprised of a steel glass, a spoon, a bed-sheet, a quilt-cover, a pillow cover, a dustbin, a dust-picker and a bucket.

I took my stuff and my luggage and proceeded towards my room. Many people were doing the same.

I opened the room's lock with the key that I was given at the reception. The room's door opened wide and I took my first step in. The view of the room was exciting.

'Wow! Bunk beds'. I had always wanted to sleep in bunk beds. It was like a small dream coming true for me. That too in just one step in the room. The adventure had just begun.

There were four bunk beds in sets of two each. I occupied one of the upper bunk beds. There were four cupboards, a chair, a table, a bathroom and the room had a balcony too. Balcony was my second favourite thing about this room. The balcony looked over to a beautiful view of the mountains towards the east and allowed a pleasant waft of air to come into the room.

I kept my luggage on the floor and I opened the door to the balcony. This is where I found my third favourite thing about this room, the trees and the greenery. Though the view outside balcony was visible from inside the room, but standing in the balcony, I could see the greenery around better. The stems of trees were hanging in the balcony and there was greenery all around. I was falling more and more in love with this room. Heaven was within my reach already.

"Is there anyone in the room?" The voice broke my day-dream and I went back inside the room from the balcony to see who it was. I saw the same tall girl with long legs, dark complexion, beautiful facial features and an athletic body peeping inside the door.

"No, there is no one in the room," I replied with a smile.

"Except me, of course".

She laughed back and asked, pointing towards the other upper bunk bed, "Has anyone taken this bed?"

"No. Not yet."

"Cool. I am claiming this one then," she said and went out to bring her luggage. Soon, her voice came from the outside of the door, "Oh, I am Kritika, by the way."

Kritika, the tall girl, joined me as my first roommate. There was a sense of freedom in her personality which made her distinct from everyone which I could sense on our first meet. Though she was shuffling her feet when I saw her the first time, she didn't appear to me as the nervous type, but a confident and a bold girl.

"I am from Hyderabad," she said introducing herself. "I have a trekking company and for that I wanted to do advance courses in mountaineering to get a better idea of this field".

"Wow, a company. Well, I love trekking too. Since always, I guess. I just didn't know for a little while. I remember when I completed the Dharamshala-Triund trek. I was pretty young at the time. But I was very excited. I was twenty four years old at that time and I..."

"Twenty four at that time... what is your age?"

"Twenty eight years". I knew what was coming.

"No ways. You look twenty three... twenty four at most". She replied with a surprised look on her face.

I smiled and tried to believe what she had said. People had told me that many times, but I never believed it. Actually, I knew I wasn't really the beautiful or young type. I was born matured.

"Have a look at the balcony. It's beautiful". I told her and we went out to see the view.

We kept conversing with each other in balcony, like we knew each other from a long time. She told me about her family and I told her about mine. We discussed about our trekking expeditions till date and shared our experiences.

It was one p.m. now and we realized that it was lunch time. We were told at the reception, the lunch times were strict and we will have to finish our lunch within that time. We took our glasses and moved out towards the food mess. The mess was near the boys hostel which was at a small walking distance. We walked through the steep road which turned towards the boys' hostel. Crossing the boy's hostel, we reached the mess.

Lunch was being served in a queue as we reached. There were sets of tables and chairs in the mess hall. I and Kritika awaited for our turn in the queue. We took the food and took chairs to sit on.

"Why do they have the mess near the boy's hostel? Don't you think this is gender disparity? Do they think only boys feel hungry?", she asked, with mild heat in voice.

I could sense she was also a feminist like me and I found it a very positive quality for us to bond as friends.

"Well, I think they believe that girls are stronger and can walk this distance. So, you should take it positively," I said with a laugh.

"Very smart. I believe you are right," she said and we high-fived with a laugh.

A girl had just taken her food and had headed with her lunch plate towards the table where we were seated. We saw the girl and saw that she was alone.

"Hi. Have a seat. I am Kritika."

"Hi. My name is Neeti. I just reached to join the course and decided to have lunch first. It feels like it has been ages since I last ate. Which room are you guys in? I have been allotted room number five," she said all of it in one breath and placed her plate in front of her chair and smiled.

"What a coincidence? We are also in room number five," Kritika replied excitedly.

She was fair, very polite and sophisticated in the manner she spoke. But many times, I have found it difficult to gel in with people who are so sophisticated. 'It will be difficult for me to handle so much sophistication. Wait. Don't be judgmental, you have just met her.' I had a flow of thoughts.

"Oh. Nice. I am glad that I met you people here" Her voice caught my attention and brought me back. She had a nice and relaxed smile. Her looks were very controlled but soft. "I am working as Lieutenant in Indian Navy. So, I have had a huge share of water in my life till now. I took this break to scale mountains because that has been one of the loves of my life since I was a kid."

I had a quick look at her again... 'Wow! She is in the Navy'. This adventure was getting more and more interesting every minute. I don't know what it holds.

Eight

"You have to be back here at the institute by six in the evening. Rules are strict, so no excuses will be accepted. And, very importantly, we have eyes around. So, no smoking and drinking even outside of the premises. Got it?" The person-in-charge had given instructions before to most of us.

The rest of the day was spent at leisure and we were given permission to go out to bring any necessary stuff that we might want from the market.

"Are you both coming with me?" Kritika and Neeti were lying on their bunk beds.

"Not today. It was a very tiring day. I want to relax now. Definitely next time though". Kritika was looking sleepy already.

"Sure. The market is nice here they say. So, I just thought of giving it a look. What about you, Neeti?", I asked her again.

"I am coming with you. Just give me five minutes". I wasn't expecting Neeti to go with me either.

"Okay."

"Sure you don't want to go?" I asked Kritika

"Yaar, really. My feet are aching after this day's work out. I need rest, else I won't be able to get up on time for the day tomorrow." She made a tired face.

"What workout?" She was with us the whole time she reached here. What workout did she do?

"Yaar. The walk from the gate to institute was no less than a workout". She said with a funny face and I laughed.

"Okay... Okay... Is there anything you want me to bring from the market?"

"Bring a cheese pizza if you can." She replied with a spark on her face.

"Okay. I will try". I smiled.

Soon Neeti and I left for the market. There is floating market in the Dal Lake that everyone talked about. I had heard a lot about it many-a-times from my maasi too and wished to visit it someday. So availing the opportunity and paying a visit there today was an excellent option for a dull day, full of lying idle and feeling homesick.

"Bhaiya. We want to go around the floating market". I asked the Shikara wala whose Shikara looked like the most beautiful one on the banks of Dal Lake.

Shikara is a kind of boat that is used to ride around the lake in Kashmir. Like Venice has their Gondolas, Kashmir has beautiful Shikaras.

"Yes madam. You can go on my Shikara. You can go around the lake and also shop in the market". Shikara-wala bhaiya told us excitedly.

It seemed that he had found a few customers that day. Though it felt like a weird thought because his Shikara was the most beautiful Shikara in the world. At least I thought so. We enquired about the Shikara ride charges and decided to experience it.

The view of the Dal Lake was a peaceful one. In the vast lake with the cool breeze blowing around, the sound of the boat rowing and boat oars striking the water gently. It looked like a dream come true; a heaven.

'How can this place be violent?' Again the thought rang in my head. It is such a beautiful place. I found it very difficult to imagine it to be one of the prominent places under terrorist attack.

We decided to do our shopping once our training was over. We could not shop and increase our luggage at the moment. It'll be increasing dead weight on us that's of no use for now. Neeti too agreed to my point of view, so we dropped the idea of shopping now.

"Madam, this is the famous Kashmiri embroidery shop. You will get beautiful suits, shawls, and carpets here," Shikara-wala bhaiya informed us.

"We will just have a view of market for now. No buying,." I told him.

"Ok...Ok, madam. You are from the mountain institute. Definitely next time. You will love the stuff here," He said as we proceeded further.

"What is your name?"

"Madam, my name is Abdul".

"So Abdul what do you do apart from Shikara riding? Do you study?"

"Madam, I wanted to study but had to leave studies to earn money for my family. But these days tourism is also not at its peak. So, it is difficult to make both ends meet sometimes". He looked like a young sixteen years old.

"I wish the situations here get better and people like you should earn. Kashmir is such a beautiful place. It attracts tourists from all over the world. But just because of the situation here, people hesitate to come. The problems disrupt the whole atmosphere and people living here."

"You are right madam. People from different parts of world come here. You see that house boat?", he was pointing his finger towards a beautiful houseboat, "this houseboat is owned by a Spanish lady. She came here once and fell in love with this place. Now she comes here every year and stays in her houseboat for two or three months. If there was more peace here, so many people could have enjoyed the beauty of nature."

"Wow, I had no idea. This is amazing. I too wish to have a houseboat experience once," Neeti suddenly jumped into the conversation. Till now, she was dreamily looking around.

The shikara was about to reach the banks and I was desperately looking around to breathe in all the beauty of this place that I could. Suddenly, someone standing at a distance caught my attention.

'Vedant? No way. This must be a dream. He cannot be here, can he? This is something I was not expecting'. My mind would have been playing tricks on me, so I blinked my eyes to come out of this dream. But he was still there. This was not a dream. He was there and was not going away from me like I thought he would. I wanted to move on and instead he just came to make my problems worse.

I kept looking at him, like a dream, not knowing how to react. The shikara turned its direction to park at the bank and I lost him in the small crowd that was there. 'Was it really him? Maybe I was indeed dreaming of him'. I thought again, looking here and there. But I could not find him anywhere.

I did not realize when I got off the Shikara and Neeti made the payments to the Shikara waala. My eyes were trying to find him again. I wanted to go near him and talk to him. I wanted to hug him and tell him that I still loved him and was so incomplete without him. At the same time, I wanted him to stay away too; to just pass by him and never notice. It was very difficult to know what I wanted.

A drop of rain fell on my face bringing me back from my thoughts. 'Was it my tear or a rain drop?' The thought made me almost rub my eyes when another drop of rain fell on my face.

"It's raining, Taara. We should hurry up and go back to the hostel". Neeti had not realized my state of mind at that time.

"Huh? Yes. Yes, we should. We should go. I should not be here..."

Nine

"You both are fully drenched". Kritika looked at us, as we entered the room.

"It's raining outside, dear. Didn't you see?"

"Oh. I did not realize that. I guess I passed out. You both must be feeling cold. You should change your clothes. Should I get you anything?"

"Yeah, we will change the clothes. That's what we are going to do. But we could not bring your pizza. It started raining. Rain here is really cold".

"That is fine. No worries".

We were taking out the clothes from our bags to change when there was a sudden knock at the door. Ginni, our fourth roommate had arrived.

A typical Gujarati girl with big eyes and an 'Arrrre' slang in her manner of speaking. I could judge this from her first words as she introduced herself. She was wearing green coloured coat with a monkey cap. It looked like she had entered into a snow zone or a glacier. She wasn't drenched as such… just some water on her cap.

"Arrre… only lower beds are vacant? I wanted the upper one". She said making a disappointed face. She kept her bags on the vacant bed and took out her face wash.

"Its seven pm and it's our dinner time. Let's go. I am feeling so hungry". Kritika announced.

"You guys go ahead. I will just wash my face and will join you at the mess itself," Ginni told us and entered the bathroom.

"Okay. Do you know the direction to the mess?", Kritika asked in a higher voice so she could hear inside the bathroom.

"Yes. I do. I am coming from there itself. I had tea there in the evening and had to wait there for the rain to stop," Ginni informed.

"Oh, okay. Poor you," Kritika said with a concerned expression.

All three of us, I, Kritika and Neeti picked up our glasses, spoons, water bottles and left for the mess. The stay here was again and again reminding me of my old hostel days.

I was in love with the sea. I always thought of holidays at beaches. I felt the serene sense of depth of life from the depth of sea. I always underrated the mountains. But since the time I met Vedant, my perception about the mountains changed. He loved mountains and like his every other liking, I started to like the mountains too. In fact, the mountains, directly or indirectly, played an important role in our story. They were the reason for us to know each other for the very first time. We had made so many memories and future dreams associated with mountains.

He dreamed to spend his life in mountains and living in a wooden house. Now that we are away from each other, I have also fallen in love with mountains. I feel the need to go to the mountains again and again. As I go close to them, they also start talking to me. They tell me about myself, bring me near to my soul. The echo of my voice in the mountains brings my own thoughts back to my heart. As I reach the heights, I feel I am coming closer to the clouds. Then I want to reach at higher heights where I can see the sky meeting the sea, everything blue and pure and unhindered, everything blended in serenity and love that can soothe any anxious soul and make me feel the real happiness. It feels like I am quenching my thirst to know about myself.

Every dream that we had was now gone with him. But this one happiness wasn't spoilt by the pain and I feel closer to everything I want, just by being in a mountainous place.

Kritika and Neeti were chatting throughout the way to the mess while I was just smiling at the direct questions only. My mind wandering off with my memories.

Ten

VEDANT

The days in the college were passing after the ragging incident. The college authorities had made strict rules against raging, so sinking into a new routine wasn't difficult at all. First year wasn't very hectic on us and soon, I got to spend time with many new classmates.

Vedant was in the senior-most batch of my department. We crossed and smiled at each other many times in the college corridors. We didn't actually talk to each other after that day. But I felt a special bond with him as if I knew him and he was not a stranger.

Meanwhile, I was getting acquainted with the college and I was getting closer to my hostel roommate and my first friend in the college, Varsha.

Though, as usual, the college friends had started making fun of us and calling us 'Taara Sitaara' as we were mostly together in college and hostel. Poor Varsha; she had to endure that because of me. However, our friendship was blossoming and we left no chance to go outside the hostel to eat, shop, loiter and have fun.

But it was quite annoying for the warden of the hostel. Our warden was a Punjaban lady with a dimpled smile. We could either see her eating something or complaining that she was not losing weight. It was fun to be with her most of the time. She stayed on the ground floor of our hostel. She was sweet but very strict about the hostel rules.

"Hey the college is taking a trip to Mussoorie," announced Varsha as she entered the room a hot summer afternoon.

"Wow, who told you?", I asked with a tone of excitement.

"Stupid… such things are posted on the notice board. I got to know from there. College has planned this one day trip before the summer vacations," Varsha informed. "After examinations".

"It's going to be fun".

"Yes".

We went back to the college to know the details of the trip and other formalities. We did not want to get late and lose this opportunity. Having to go out and have fun was an altogether awesome opportunity before going back home.

We slumped during examinations and most of us had our necks deep in books. They were the only stressful days in the hostel. Whenever the exam was just on the next day, most of the students could be seen cramming in the hallway, mess and almost everywhere. But those days would pass as soon as they could.

Finally, the day came and we were all ready for the trip.

"Hurry up, yaar. We are already late. The buses will leave the college and we will be left out," I told Varsha who was still packing her bag. "It's just one day anyway. Let's just go."

"Yes. It's almost done," she said hurriedly as she packed the dabba of namkeen and sweets that her mother had sent her from home a few days back

As we reached the college, we were already late. Two buses had already left and there was just one bus waiting. We climbed on the bus. Varsha found a seat to sit.

However, I had to keep standing, looking for some place to sit in the bus. Varsha was also looking around to find a seat for me. But the bus looked full.

"The bus is almost full. You will not find a seat here. You come with me. We will go by the college van." I looked around to see Rekha ma'am. She was one of our college's faculties. I followed her to the van.

I saw Vedant and another guy already sitting in the van.

"This is Vedant and that is Sarvesh. They are helping me in coordinating this trip. You can come with us in this van," Rekha ma'am informed as I took my seat next to Sarvesh. Me, Sarvesh and Vedant were sitting on the middle seat and Rekha mam was sitting with one more faculty member in one of the back seats.

Sarvesh, me and Vedant starting conversing with each other. It was the first time that I was conversing with Vedant and I could see some strange happiness in his eyes too, as if he felt a bond with me too. Vedant enquired about me a bit. He was keen to know more about me, my family but he seemed a bit shy. I could sense that. Amid all the talks, I did not realize when we reached Mussoorie.

Varsha joined me as soon as we reached there. Her bus had reached before us and she was waiting for me. We had a great time in Mussoorie. Kempty Falls was the main attraction.

But my thoughts remained stuck on Vedant. The way he talked, he smiled and shied away but kept on asking questions was repeatedly coming to me like I was still living in that moment. Suddenly meeting Vedant and getting to know him more was making this trip more enjoyable. Though we parted ways once we reached Mussoorie, but we kept exchanging glances with each other.

The mountains had never felt so beautiful to me earlier. I think there was love in the air that was making them even more spectacular to me. Vedant seemed so excited as he was clicking the pictures. I wanted to look at him, but at the same time, I was also fearful of getting caught red handed looking at a handsome guy and wanted to avoid the embarrassment.

'Is he also feeling the same?' The question was being raised incessantly in my mind as I had found him looking at me too every now and then.

I secretly wished to go back to college again with him in the college van. But Varsha had already reserved a seat for me in the bus this time and I had to accompany her.

The summer vacations were starting the next day and I was going back to hostel in the bus. My bus for home was early the next morning and so I knew I wasn't going to see him again till the end of the summer. It was a weird feeling in the pit of my stomach, like the holidays were ending. The feeling of not being able to see Vedant for so many days was making me sad.

Eleven

MOUNTAINEERING INSTITUTE

We had reached the mess for dinner and were in the food queue with all the participants. The food had both veg and non-veg options. Egg was served in non-veg. While there was a dal, sabzi, vegetable salad, roti and rice for the vegetarians. Being a non-veg lover, I was not bothered about which dal and which sabzi like most of the participants there. I took some egg curry, roti, rice and took my seat on the table.

The thought of seeing Vedant in Kashmir was still lingering in my mind off and on. 'Was it my dream or was he really there?' I was lost in my thoughts while eating. It felt weird because no matter what, I haven't ever hallucinated of him before.

"The food is nice na?" asked Neeti, tasting the aloo matar. "Hey I am asking you. Where are you lost?"

"Huh? Oh sorry. I thought you were asking Kritika. Yes it's good. However, I don't know about the aloo matar," I replied, coming out of my thoughts.

"What happened? You are lost in your thoughts since we have come back from market. Is anything wrong?" She had seen me staring at nothing everywhere, so she seemed concerned.

"No, no. Everything is good. I am just a bit tired, nothing else," I replied, trying to cover up my expressions.

Many other participants, from all over India, had joined at the mess this time. Some were sitting with us at our dinner table too. Neeti had blocked a chair for Ginni as we used to in school and hostel. Many things were happening at this time of my life which reminded me of the best days of my life: 'The Hostel days'.

We introduced ourselves to our new friends Aryan, Abhishek and Manav at the mess table and interacted with them. They were from different fields and all of them shared their passion for mountains.

"Basically, people come here for this course under three criterions, sponsored ones, army or navy or any other defence personnel and the private participants". Aryan knew a lot and told a lot too.

"I think I will come under the private participant category," I told everyone.

"Yes and I am the sponsored one," Kritika said and smiled to everyone.

"What is that?" Neeti asked.

"See, those participants, whose course is sponsored by some government or private institutes are the sponsored participants," Kritika informed further.

"And in your case, being a Navy person, you were sponsored by Navy. There are many who are from army or other defence backgrounds," Aryan added.

Ginni had finally joined us for dinner.

"It took you so long to wash your face?" said Neeti with a teasing smile.

Ginni smiled back and started having her dinner.

"Hey, we were discussing about the types of participants here," Kritika said

"I am a private one," Ginni replied instantly interrupting Kritika like the smart kid in the class. We laughed.

"Yes, I was about to ask that only," Kritika laughed too.

Soon we left dinner and bid good night to each other.

Back at our room, we started setting our beds. Unlike home, here we had to do everything ourselves and it felt really good to finally get some time to sleep.

"How do you cover the quilts with these quilt covers?" Kritika was struggling with her quilt cover still.

"Right? They are so small," Ginni seconded her. They both were struggling with their quilt covers. Neeti and I laughed at them as we saw they had themselves in the cover and were holding quilts the wrong side up.

"It's very easy. Let me help you out," I replied like a quilt cover expert and climbed down my bed to help them. I tried my hand in it and spoiled the whole thing even more.

"You sounded as if you have been covering the quilts since ages and now see what you have done?", Kritika said with sarcastic laugh.

"Yeah. I was also thinking that", Ginni joined her and laughed louder. I could not hold back my laughter either. Soon, we were all were giggling and trying to get the quilts in the covers.

"Let me try again from the start," Ginni said and took the quilt cover from me. We had finally recovered from our laughing fit and decided to complete the work faster.

She finally succeeded in covering her quilt and shared the quilt covering technique with Kritika. All four quilts had their covers on them. All of us high fived happily after the completion of this 'Quilt Cover Mission'.

The knock at the door interrupted the quilt cover session going on in our room. Neeti went to open the door. We saw our instructor along with other institute members standing at the door. He informed us about the schedule which was going to be followed in the coming days.

"The first bell will ring at five a.m. to wake you all up. You can go to mess and have your morning tea. At six a.m., there will be 'Fall In', which means you have to gather for PT in the PT area. You will get acquainted with all these terms in coming days. For now, 'Fall in'. After PT, you can go have your breakfast at eight a.m.. There will be one hour of free time after that for you to get ready. After this, everyday's schedule will be displayed on notice board, depending on what you have to do. So you got to check that every day. Got it?"

"Yes, sir."

"And one more important thing, all lights should be off by nine p.m. every day. It is important for the mountaineers to sleep well at night. This needs to be followed very strictly". He smiled and left the room along with other institute members who were here for the instructions.

"I think we are going to enjoy the stay here. Life will start tomorrow. Yay...," Ginni closed the door and expressed her joy with a fun shout.

"Yes, the way we enjoyed the hostel days," I said and everyone agreed to my view.

As the beds had been set by now, we started interacting about each other's hostel life experiences. While Ginni and Kritika were talking so much, I couldn't help but notice how introverted Ginni was. With her gujju slang, she said many things but I could see that she was actually quite an introvert person who tried to be and look like an extrovert. She was listening to everyone and sharing a bit too. But her anxiety was visible.

It was nine at night and already it was time to sleep. I climbed on my upper bunk bed and applied a pain relief gel that I bought from the market for the injury from the fall on railway station. 'The instructors had no idea… I exactly know what 'fall in' was'. I smiled at my own word pun as Neeti switched off the lights. Soon, we all slept to wake up early and see our dreams getting fulfilled the next day.

Twelve

Next Day

The bell rang after what seemed like ten minutes of sleeping. But really it was five on the watch. 'How could it be?' The sound of the bell was loud enough to wake me and all of us up from the deep sleep.

'Thank God! The sound of bell was soothing.'

It looked like it was coming from a distance with a little echo. Or else it'd have been a kick for the new morning. As I peeled off my quilt and got up, I saw Ginni in front of the mirror looking herself from side to side adjusting her cap.

"Hey, good morning." She gazed through the mirror reflection as she saw me looking at her.

"Good Morning. Were you up even before the bell?" I asked, yawning.

"Just a little. You will have nashta na?"

"Nashta...? I thought we will be getting only tea at this time."

"Yeah I meant tea. We call it nashta in Gujarat," she laughed sheepishly.

"Okay. No, I will not have tea". Nodding, she left to go to mess with her glass. Neeti and Kritika were not in the room either.

‘Wow. Only I waited for the bell to ring’. Getting down from the bed I got ready for PT. Suddenly, the view from the balcony caught my eyes and the large lush green field surrounded by the trees just mesmerized me. ‘This is why I love this.’

I had done a few treks before, but never saw such beautiful green velvet carpet of nature spread over such a large area. I never imagined that nature could be so beautiful in some places. But nature was beautiful in most places. It was us who ruined the beauty.

It seemed that the field was filled with water as a number of swans could be seen fluttering in.

‘Oh yeah, it had rained yesterday night’. I had a quick thought. Hundreds of milky white swans were dipping their beaks in the water on the grass and were moving around. The swans seemed like white spots on a green carpet and were adding so much to the beauty, especially when seen from a distance.

I wanted to capture this moment. I ran inside for my camera. These days when you think about a camera, you think about your mobile phone. Everything is packed inside this rectangular device these days.

‘Spending one day without a mobile phone has become difficult now’. I had promised myself to keep the use of mobile to the minimum on this trip. But I had to use it every now and then. Checking time was one of the major hurdles which brought me close to the mobile again and again, of course. Now, I can guess taking pictures can be added to the list.

‘I should have brought a wrist watch… and a camera’. I captured the beautiful moment in my camera…well my mobile and updated pictures in my family group.

Ping.

"I am indeed jealous of you right now," Pranay replied instantly.

I was surprised to see him awake this early in the morning.

"I will bring a swan for you".

I replied with a laughing smiley. I knew it was hard for him to hold back his excitement. I took a few selfies with the breath-taking view in the background and sent it to mom. I knew she was eagerly waiting for my pictures here. I updated a few pictures on my social media account too. This is one thing that we all do as a normal part of our lives these days. We give people a peek into our lives through our eyes now and then.

Ping.

'*Beautiful.... Background...*' I got the first comment from a school friend with a teasing smiley.

Thirteen

The mountaineering regime was starting today with PT. The walk to the PT area was easy, refreshing and definitely cold. The breeze touched my cheeks and I felt both cold and refreshed. I put on my jacket fast and started walking faster. I was holding my hands together and rubbed the back of them when I suddenly stopped in my tracks.

'What's wrong with me? Why am I seeing him again and again? Do I need a psychiatrist?' I thought and forcefully blinked my eyes. I looked at a few people around and looked back at the place I saw him earlier, thinking like a memory, he would disappear now. But he was still there. Yes, Vedant was there. He was standing there with his hands in his jacket's pockets and was looking around. My body froze, not with the cold but with the uncertainty. I didn't know whether I should just duck… or run away. I had no idea how to take the decision.

But before my body could do, the decision was taken for me. He was scanning the background and soon, his eyes met mine. Shock registered on his face as he double checked if it was me. Like me, he was in shock too. He had no idea he'd see me here.

It felt like an unsure dream coming true. I was not sure whether I wanted him back in my life again. My heart wanted him back but my mind was totally against it. A part of me wanted to go running towards him, hug him and tell him that I still dream about him; while the other part was warning me to stay away from him. I felt like a firefly near fire, enchanted. It knew it was about to get hurt, but still had no control over itself.

An absolute mess was manifesting in my mind and my heart. As I was juggling between the thoughts, or my thoughts of disbelief, of Vedant's presence and the desire to meet him, the PT teacher's voice brought me back to reality.

"All's in mind". The voice echoed in my ears which seemed like some heavenly forecast of the mental status that I was in at that moment. This heavenly forecast helped me to come back from my thoughts and gave me time to think and react. I walked near the class assembly and stood aloof from everyone, within everyone.

"Hello, I am Rajeev Sharma. I have climbed Mount Everest twice as well as many other high-altitude mountain peaks across the world that I am sure many of you aspire to set foot on someday. I am sixty years old and I am going to be your fitness instructor for the coming days."

"Sixty years old… and so fit," Neeti exclaimed out loud and everyone around her heard it.

"Yes, miss. Sixty years and so fit. I told you all this so you can try and keep up with me". Many students smiled and the instructor continued, "The most important thing I would like to share from my mountaineering as well as life experience is that everything is in the mind. If you train your mind, you can face the biggest problems very easily. So, when I tell you to be strong, it means both physically and mentally. Be the master of your mind because you never lose a battle if your mind keeps fighting. First, you give up on a thing mentally then the defeat follows. So, learn to master your mind, your thoughts and be your self-motivator. No one can motivate you the way your mind can motivate yourself. This is going to be a very useful tip for you for the coming days".

I saw Vedant and he was looking at me with a smile of being pleasantly surprised, but it had easily settled on his lips. The same smile that used to take my heart away a couple of years back. Surprise was that it still had the power to do so. He was not looking tensed at all. He suddenly looked happier.

Though the restless eyes had lost their innocence and there was a shade of worry. Maybe the worry of being lost in the world. There was an expression of the fear of losing oneself and anxiety of not knowing what was wrong in life. I could still feel his heart and could read his eyes. Or maybe just the reflection of my own feelings.

'There was a time when his eyes spoke to my heart. But at that time, his words tore my soul. He was the one who introduced me to the feeling of love. But he was the only one who helped me know the feeling of a heartbreak also. I cannot let this happen to me again. I cannot go through that pain… again. I could not even recover from it all these years. I cannot touch that wound again which threatens to bleed again and again. It would be best if I avoided him'. My mind was racing as the sixty-year-old instructor was telling more of his experiences.

"So now you know." Instructor's voice pulled me back into the present as he continued. "We will now start our day with the PT and body stretch exercises."

We proceeded for a five-kilometre run after the exercises. Starting from the PT area and moving uphill towards the gate of the institute, we passed by the institute gate, past the zoo and came out of the main gate. I was tired already but determined to complete the run.

The greenery, beautiful flowers, small green plants… everything was so beautiful. I was trying to keep my mind on admiring the beauty around the road but the encounter with

Vedant was flashing through my mind. The more I was trying to avoid him, the more I wanted to have a glance of him again. The fight was going on between my heart and mind and I was tearing inside. This was going to be a beautiful trip. A special trip. But....

Fourteen

"Is anything cooking between you and that guy Vedant?" Varsha had caught up to me.

"Huh… Why what happened?"

"His friend Sarvesh was telling me that he really likes you and you both met on the Mussorrie trip?" Varsha told me with a question tone. "If he is lying, you should most definitely confront him."

"Umm…," I said nothing and smiled at her.

"So it's true? Or, are you mad at me?" Her pitch went a notch higher.

"Why?"

"Oh my God! I do not believe this. He is not meant for a decent girl like you, Taara. He keeps standing outside college most of the time with his friends, always bunking classes. He struggles to pass his exams and you are among the toppers of the college. I have also heard that he drinks too".

"But still I like him. There is something about him which attracts me towards him. It feels like he is meant to be mine". Varsha gave me a fuming look. "Okay okay. I will stay away from him. Now smile," I tried assuring her. But my heart was dancing with happiness. Of all the conversations I had with

Varsha, the news that Vedant likes me was thrilling me with that 'butterflies in my stomach' kind of feeling.

I was not one of those persons who are attracted towards someone at first sight. I always thought that the man of my dreams would be intelligent and smart. I never got attracted to men just because of their looks. But this time it was different. Vedant had stirred the silent distinct cords of my heart which I had no idea about. He had made me forget about all the parameters that I had set for my prince charming. It seemed like I actually wanted him and it doesn't matter what he is.

I wanted to be in a relationship for the first time. Never before had I tasted of this side of mine. I was one of the toppers, the top five students who were selected all over New Delhi for admission in the best college in India. So, I was here in Dehradun at one of the best colleges for engineering in India. I had dreams of being an efficient engineer. The same dream which I knew remained unfulfilled for my father. I knew his love for this profession and I wanted to fulfil this dream for him. As soon as I got the chance to choose a career, I thought about nothing else but becoming a mechanical engineer. I prepared for it and was so focused towards my goal that I never got time to see the handsome guys in my school or anywhere around. Even the ones who had shown interest in me, drifted away soon because of my ignorant attitude towards them. I did not want any distraction from the goal that I wanted to achieve.

I knew what Varsha said about Vedant was mostly true. Then, what's wrong with me? Why am I not able to think better? Why does my heart not agree to ignore him? He is not even the type of guy I thought I would like… ever. I was myself surprised with my behaviour. It felt as if a new person that was sleeping inside me had suddenly awakened and was making choices for me. Like somehow, the Taara that existed till now… has finally retired and gave way for this girl she had no idea would take over her.

Fifteen

Soon the physical task was over and it was breakfast time. I was supposed to be hungry after all the exercise and PT but strangely I was not. My mind was still stuck on Vedant. Vedant turned towards the girls' lot, maybe to look for me, but I had made my way out. My mind was not ready to confront the mess that had come up. So, walking away felt like the right answer.

"Hi." Suddenly his voice came from behind me and my heart skipped a beat. I wanted to run fast so I could create a lot of distance between us, but my legs were not helping me. I wanted to fake a smile and tell him that I didn't want to talk to him, but my mouth wasn't giving me help either.

"Hi." Suddenly his voice was just behind me and in the next step, he was in front of me. He was smiling.

"Hi". My lips couldn't manage a smile back.

"How are you and what are you doing here? I mean I am so surprised to see you here. A pleasant surprise though. Very pleasant." He paused to catch hold of his breath. It seemed he had walked fast or had run a bit to talk to me.

"Ummm... I am here for this mountaineering course. I guess that's why you are here too."

Vedant knew the Taara who was not keen on mountaineering at the time. This passion developed when we had already parted ways. He always wanted to live in the mountains. But I was the one who always wanted to go to the beaches. Maybe I started loving the mountains because being close to the mountains reminded me of him. Maybe the way my heart felt alive in the mountains was because of him.

"I mean I just wanted to explore this side of mine". I hid or tried to hide the void he had created in my life.

"Hmm... I too wanted to do this course. I think I told you too about it, right?"

"Sorry. I don't remember that". '*Taara... someday I'll definitely go to take that course. You will be there with me, right?*' His voice was echoing in my head. I could forget his words? "How's everyone at home?"

"Everyone is fine. I have joined Dad's business and trying to fulfil my dreams on the side. I wish to climb Mount Everest after this. You remember?"

"Umm…"

"Of course. You just said you don't."

"I was heading towards the mess. My friends are waiting there. Bye for now". Any more steps down this road will take me down the rabbit hole. I turned towards the mess and tried running away fast.

"Oh… Okay." It seemed that he wanted to say something more but he stopped himself.

As I ran away, suddenly I felt his breath was high as he had run to me, while mine was high because I ran away from him.

Sixteen

"Our real examination will start in a few days, and only then we will move to the base camp". Kritika was sipping her tea. "Hello…?"

"Huh...Yes? Sorry, I didn't hear you. What did you say?"

"What happened? I can clearly see the worry on your face".

"No. Nothing. Everything is fine."

"Are you sure? You are not looking good. Why were you late to mess? You can share it with me if there is some problem. For now, we are families to each other".

I smiled at her. "Thanks, dear. But everything is well".

"Okay... Then sip your tea and enjoy this awesome weather. Your tea is already getting cold". She placed her cup suddenly on the table. "By the way, you saw that chocolaty guy who was there during the exercises. The one who went in front to teach a few exercises too. He is my new crush."

"Huh…" The colour must have drained from my face as I recovered quickly. "Really? You liked him?"

"Yes. I am just wondering what his name is. I want to know more about him". She winked at me.

I tried laughing, but since it didn't work, I stuffed my mouth with the breakfast. However, Kritika saw my face and read something.

"Tell me, Taara. Please. It will help."

"I, I saw Vedant today. My ex".

"Here… Is he taking the course too?"

"Yes."

"Bad break up?"

I didn't know how to answer the question, but she didn't need one. "Oh so, you are scared that you will fall in love with him again?"

"Maybe I am in love with him. I don't want to be."

Kritika could feel the anxiety in my voice. She wrapped her long arms around me. Her eyes were sincere when she said what she said next, "I think you should face your fears. The more you will keep running from them, the more they will haunt you. I think you should try to feel as if whatever happened was in the past and it should not affect your present. Focus on this course, Taara. Focus on what you want to do. Do not resist your feelings. Take control of them."

"Hmmm, I think you are right."

"Only someday you'll feel that I am right. Till then, hang in there. Let's go to the camp. Enough of the mental stress. We are going to have an adventurous day today."

She had a habit of changing the topic when she felt she had nothing valuable to add in a situation. I had noticed this earlier too. I smiled and we headed toward the camp area.

Seventeen

"Will you accompany me to meet Vedant in a restaurant?", I asked Varsha very hesitantly. I knew she didn't like Vedant at all.

"What? Why do you have to meet him?" Varsha looked up from her book.

"Yaar, please understand. Sarvesh came to me yesterday when I was standing in the college corridor. He said that Vedant really likes me and wants to meet me. He has requested to meet him once".

"Taara, you promised me that you will stay away from him. He is not good".

"Yes, I remember yaar. But I really like him and I can feel that he likes me too. What is the harm in meeting him once? I need you by my side at this time. Please come with me."

"Oh, God. Love is really blind. But your love is deaf and dumb and weird and..."

"I get it. Please come".

"I guess so is mine for you."

"Yay. You are such a sweetheart. I love you, yaar". I hugged her and kept the beautiful blue top on the bed that I thought I'd wear to go see Vedant.

"Yes. Wear this. You'll look good."

Next evening, we reached the restaurant near our college as decided. Vedant was already there, waiting for us at the table that he had booked. He looked so handsome in his black shirt and jeans... casual and yet so amazing. The shape of his biceps could be seen from the shirt itself. I was amazed at the feelings that were rising in my mind. The most handsome guy of the college liked me.

"Hi". He seemed nervous by his tone. I was making him nervous. He had come alone. We sat in front of him.

"Hi". Varsha didn't open her mouth. But she definitely liked what she saw. That gave me a little satisfaction and proud. "She is my friend Varsha."

"Yes. I have seen you both together mostly in college. You both seem to be very close friends."

"We are". Varsha replied before I could.

The waiter had come to take our order. Though I am a huge foodie, but my stomach was full of butterflies. I did not order much, I did not know if Vedant would like a foodie girlfriend. So, I ordered a coffee for myself. Vedant and Varsha also ordered a coffee and a sandwich.

"Taara, I know it may feel a bit weird to a studious girl like you to meet someone like me".

"No. Nothing like that".

"Well, I do understand the situation. But I just want to know you more closely," he said, a bit hesitant.

"I think I'll go and use the washroom. Meanwhile, maybe you will feel better and talk to her better". Varsha had felt that Vedant was feeling hesitant to talk in front of her. She got up, and to my surprise, smiled at Vedant. She soon turned to the washroom.

"Taara, I do not want to pressure you into any decision. I just want you to know me too. There is something about you which no one has. I am never attracted to anyone the way I am attracted to you. You, just, are really different from everyone. You are…"

He stopped talking as he was expecting me to say something, while I was feeling very shy to reply. I was just nodding and listening to him.

"You do not want to say anything?"

"I think you are right. There is no harm in knowing each other. We can be friends". I was trying to hide the crackers of happiness that were bursting inside my heart. "For now, this is all I can say".

The waiter had come with our order and seeing this, Varsha joined us back.

"She usually eats so less… or she is trying to impress me?" Vedant asked Varsha.

"She eats a lot. She is a huge foodie," Varsha replied making her eyes big and they both laughed.

"Oh… thank God. Now that you have revealed that about me, I can have your sandwich". I laughed and picked up a little of her sandwich.

"You can eat mine too", Vedant pushed his plate to me and I blushed.

Butterflies would never be enough for me to eat. Thank God, Varsha eased up a bit. Vedant was really amazing.

Eighteen

The schedule for the day was posted on the notice board. There was a rush of candidates for training, some noting down the schedule while some taking its picture in their mobiles. Kritika took a note of it and informed me about it. However, I told her to let it remain a suspense. I wanted the moments in this trip to be surprising for me. Not as surprising as my ex-boyfriend turning up on the scene, but a little surprising. I did not want to know everything beforehand.

"Stupid girl, if you do not know the schedule for the day, how will you prepare for it? And I think you have already got the biggest surprise or rather shock by meeting your ex. Do you really want any more surprises?" Kritika was making fun of me. But she had a point.

We reached the ground on schedule and Vedant was already there.

"Hello everyone. The most important thing to be learned in mountaineering is team spirit. As per experts in this field, the one who can face a mountain can face anything in life. But for that, we need to understand the importance of team spirit. There are many situations in mountaineering which needs a team to be working more carefully with each other, lending and taking support from each other. All the big names in this field have a record of being very good team members. After a week's training here, we will proceed to the base camp for the second phase of this course. That will be a tough exam for all. I will advise you to focus on the first phase because the techniques taught here will help you to complete the second phase without much difficulty. First phase is like the foundation. Just like the foundation of the house needs to be strong, so should your techniques. I personally do not like those candidates who do not take the first phase seriously and later have to quit the course mid-way as they find it very difficult," Rajeev sir's voice rang loudly.

The way he talked and motivated us, sent a wave of enthusiasm among us. I was refreshed with his speech and wanted to do my best.

"So, the very first thing we will do is divide you all into eight groups: the eight ropes. From now on, you will have some group activities as well as individual activities so that you learn to face situations in mountaineering both as a team and as an individual. Got it?" Everyone nodded while Mr Rajeev assessed for the formation of groups.

Rajeev Sir divided people into groups. He tried his best to form balanced groups with equal number of candidates from the army/police, sponsored and the private ones like me in each rope. I and another girl were left in the end and two ropes were left which lacked one member each. One of them was Vedant's rope.

"You two can join any one rope of your choice."

I was having mixed feelings to join Vedant's rope but before I could say anything, the other girl took her decision and I was roped into Vedant's rope. I saw him looking at me just like he was looking at the restaurant, nervous but happy. We were a team now.

"So, the first exercise is complete. As you can see, there are 5 people in each rope. Today you'll have to interact and spend time with other members. Get acquainted with each other. We are going to have an artificial wall climbing session tomorrow where we will judge you as a team and marks will be given to you. The team with the highest score will be the winner. The evening is free today. But from tomorrow, you will have a whole hour's theory class in the auditorium daily where you will be taught about all aspects and techniques to be used in mountaineering. Today, you people can go out for three hours from five to eight pm. But remember no smoking and no drinking allowed during the period of training. Going outside without permission is also not allowed. As you all know, there are two cafes in the premises. You can go there. As you people are going out today, I am reminding these rules again. They should be followed very strictly while your stay in this institute. We are calling it a day now. I will see you people tomorrow morning in the rock-climbing session."

I was in rope number four and so was Vedant and Aryan. Kritika was in rope six, Ginni and Neeti were together in rope seven. As we started interacting with one another, all the rope members came together. I already knew two of them; Aryan and Vedant. Aryan was a private teacher but martial arts trained. Abhishek was a black cat commando. He was posted at Siachin. Sujoy was pursuing Ph.D. in Bengali literature. He used Bengali slangs while talking. I was the only girl in my rope but I felt comfortable with all my ropemates as they seemed quite interactive and easy to talk to.

"You have come all the way from Kolkata?", Aryan asked Sujoy.

"Yes, dude".

"Somehow, I don't understand your combo. Ph.d. in literature and mountaineering?"

"It's just like the sweet dish combo of Gulab jamun with ice cream". Sujoy was funny and everyone laughed around him. I saw Vedant was not talking much like me.

"Do you guys know each other?" Abhishek asked Vedant as our body language was giving us away a little.

"Hmm. Yes. We were together in college". Vedant looked at me. "We do know each other".

"Ooo, that's great. You guys are already friends".

"Actually we weren't friends. Just acquaintances". I felt bad after saying it. I did not know what came over me. Vedant's expressions said he didn't like that either.

I didn't want Vedant to know that I still felt for him. Instead, I had it printed on my head in bold letters. He could read my hurt. He could see that I still had feelings for him. Feelings of hate are also feelings. Why do we forget that sometimes... most of the times?

Nineteen

I was getting to know Vedant closely now. He was a rich guy which meant that his father was very rich. But he never showed that or said a lot about it. He was pretty down to earth as such. He loved his bike a lot, which he never called a bike because it was an 'Enfield'. No one could call it a bike, and not even the most ignorant people like me, who couldn't understand the difference between a scooter and a scooty, was allowed to insult the Enfield.

Besides his bike maintenance and fuel charges, he loved to spend time on his fitness, his branded things and his drinks. It all seemed perfect for someone who loves to be pampered as a girlfriend because he showered me with a lot of gifts every now and then. Though I felt it was wastage of money, but for him, it was his way of showing his love. He was a rule breaker and one of those brats in college who were always on the teachers' most wanted list. From leaking the examination papers to breaking the hostel window panes for taking revenge from boys in the hostel, every incident involved Vedant as a highlight. I was scared earlier but the person who was in love with me was a different Vedant. It was hard for me to believe that he was a college gangster.

Mobile phones were not allowed in the hostel premises but Vedant had gifted me one. I had refused to take it but Vedant emotionally blackmailed me as he did for most of his gifts. Hostel rules were being broken by me too now. Our late night conversations had started and the more I talked, the more I got addicted to Vedant. We mostly talked when everyone had slept.

"Where are you going?" Varsha had woken up from her sleep as I accidentally dropped a glass while going out of the room at midnight.

"Umm, I am going out to talk to Vedant. I'll be back in ten minutes. You sleep".

"Okay," she groaned and covered her face, but suddenly spoke again. "Hey, wait. Outside? What if anyone comes to know that you have a mobile phone?"

The thought of me getting caught with the mobile phone woke her up. She clearly had no idea about what was going on.

"I am going to talk on the terrace", I winked. The rule breaking thing was exhilarating for me too. The model student that I was, I had never broken rules.

"Terrace? Is it open at this time?"

"Umm, I have the duplicate key," I giggled.

"Oh, Vedant," She made a face. He had never met a rule that he hadn't broken.

I nodded in agreement and moved out to talk.

Vedant was really good at talking to people. He was like a brat who was good at heart and helped people. So whenever he needed help, people would help him back. That's how he had arranged a duplicate terrace key for me.

"I have been calling you for so long. Where were you? Is everything okay?" Vedant had an anxious tone.

"Yes. What's gonna happen to me in here, Vedant? Varsha had woken up so I stopped to talk to her".

"You told her about the duplicate key?"

"Yes. She is my buddy". My hostel days had become more adventurous with Vedant in my life and I never left a day to tell him.

"Hmm"

"What happened?"

"Nothing"

"Please. Is anything wrong?"

"You do not know what is wrong?"

"No. Tell me what happened?" I felt worried.

"I had told you to keep it a secret. Then why you have to tell it to everyone that you have the duplicate key?"

"I just told Varsha. She is really important to me, Vedant. You know that."

"I know she is more important to you. More important than anyone else. But some things should be between you and me."

"Why are you making an issue about such small thing? I do not tell her everything. I just..."

"Okay. Fine. You never understand anyway. I don't like your over-protective friend. She is not good for our relationship".

"Vedant, you are mistaken. She will never come between us. She is a nice girl. Trust me."

"I think I should sleep now. Good night". He disconnected the call before I replied.

'How can he be angry on such petty issues? Is there something else that he is not telling me? I should have been more patient. Maybe he wanted to tell me something'. A number of thoughts were running in my mind. I was tossing in my bed.

'I am sorry', I messaged. 'Message delivered', the phone screen flashed.

I kept waiting for his reply but it did not come. I kept waiting and dozed off with the mobile phone in my hand.

'Hey... I had slept... I was drunk...' The message flashed on the phone screen at six a.m..

'Why do you drink so much?'

'I love you', it came with a heart smilcy.

'I love you too', I typed and paused. I deleted it. I was angry.

"We should not drink and smoke. The rules are very strict. Oh… Cheers." Kritika had taken the first beer can in her hand. Her voice brought me back from my thoughts.

"Cheeeerrsssss…." Neeti laughed and sipped.

Neeti, Ginni, Kritika and I had come out for shopping, but the first thing we did was to find a good bar and restaurant to eat and… well, drink.

"How can you guys like it?" Ginni was trying beer for the first time. She had started making faces after even smelling the beer.

"Babes, you will like it. It's your first time, that's why it tastes funny. That's it". Kritika was the Liquor Guru.

"We are breaking the rules. I have loved this feeling once". I felt a similar tugging exhilaration.

"Yes. Actually, the beer and the rule breaking, both are intoxicating". Neeti was already into her second can.

"Guys, you heard the breaking news?" Kritika's voice went a notch up.

"What news?" Ginni was avoiding her can a little bit.

"Taara's ex-boyfriend is here, in the institute". Kritika finished her second beer can. The beer was showing its effect.

"Really?", Neeti was surprised.

"Did I not tell you to keep it a secret?" I felt annoyed.

"Oops"

"Shut up. Who is it? Is it that cute chocolaty boy that Kritika is crushing on?" Ginni had downed her can now.

"Hmm, it's Vedant. We were together in college."

"You never told me that. Shit, I was really starting to like him. Now, I can't. He is your ex."

"Great. It was five years back. I did not want to see him again in my life. But now that it is happening, I am trying to avoid him as much as I can. You can have him, Kritika".

"No. Vedant is cute, yaar. But I am going to stay clear of your way."

"Yes. He is". I smiled back.

"I can understand. I have also gone through a break up. Hurts like hell". Neeti said in a sympathizing tone. "But now you both are in the same rope. It will be a difficult thing to avoid him".

"I know. I have been running away from his memories and trying to forget him. But now, it will become more difficult for me."

"Leave it. Let's not spoil this evening's fun. Let's order some food". Ginni said

"Yes, you are right. But there is a problem," Neeti said with a sympathetic tone.

"What problem?"

"You won't get dhokla here". Neeti and Kritika laughed as I was smiling.

"Haha funny. Now can we order?" Soon the three changed the subject and we ordered food. In sometime, delicious Kashmiri food was served. The evening was going on perfect. Beer, food, friends and happiness. We all entered the gate of the institute before eight pm.

We dunked into the bed. Soon Neeti and Ginni slept.

"Hey, Taara." Kritika was sounding a bit more drunk than the others.

"Yes, Kritika."

"You were trying to feel surprised by the schedule, while your life has surprised you with Vedant. Just accept that he is here. Maybe something will change. Maybe now things will make better sense".

Soon Kritika dozed off as my thoughts ran here and there. It was a good evening. Maybe she was right. Maybe, finally things will make sense.

Twenty

Soon the whole of Dehradun was witnessing our love story. The mountains, the cafes, shops, the gardens, we roamed everywhere together. Vedant pampered me in every possible way money and he could. Food, shopping, clothes and everything that I may or may not need was given to me. We bunked classes together, roamed around the city in the day and talked over the phone at night. Talking under the starry sky is one of the most romantic things I had done. Vedant and I talked till midnight and more. No Disprin was curing the hangover of this love and I was doing things I never did.

"Vedant, I am feeling so hungry". I was talking to him from the hostel terrace at midnight.

"Should I get you something to eat?", he teased.

"Yeah right. How will you do that? You very well know that you cannot enter the hostel premises at this time".

"I will give it to the hostel security guard".

"No. No. Do not do that. Warden will come to know about you and she is very clever in such matters. She will inform my parents. Leave it."

"Do not worry about all that. You just tell me what you want to eat". He sounded pretty determined.

"Ummmm. I want to have a watermelon," I joked. Of course there was less chance of finding one right now.

“Okay”. He disconnected the call without saying anything else.

“Hey, I am just kidding.” I tried to tell him but he didn’t listen and neither picked the call again.

‘It seems he was also joking’. I thought and went back to my room to sleep.

The phone flashed a message after half an hour.

‘Come to the boundary wall at the back of your hostel in 5 minutes’.

‘Oh my God! Is he bringing the watermelon? No way’.

“Varsha, get up”. I shook her and literally pushed her off the bed. “Get up yaar”

“What, what happened?” She tried to get up and run like in an emergency.

“We have to go to the back of the hostel.”

“What… back… But why?” She was rubbing her eyes confused.

“I will tell you on the way. Just come with me.”

“It surely has something to do with your mad boyfriend, right?” She was groaning and getting up from her deep sleep irritated.

“Yes”.

When we reached the back boundary wall of the hostel, Vedant had already reached.

“Taara, I have brought the watermelon you wanted to eat. I have a ladder and I am climbing the wall. Okay?”

“Okay,” I responded from other side of the wall.

In no time, I could see Vedant was on the top of the wall with a huge watermelon in his hand.

"Hi". He was smiling.

"You are mad, Vedant. I thought you were joking. But you are really mad, you know?"

"I am mad for you," he whispered looking into my eyes. He mostly ignored Varsha's presence.

"Aww… Now can we go before we are caught? I am kind of looking forward to be an engineer, you see?" Varsha was standing there looking at both of us like we were the weirdest couple in the whole world till now. I loved that look in her eyes. She was irritated and annoyed, but also a bit envious.

"Aye, who is there?" We heard the voice of security guard coming from a distance. He was coming close, running. "Wait, wait…"

"Catch the watermelon Taara. I am going," Vedant said leaving the watermelon from his hands in a hurry.

But I could not balance the water melon and it fell on the ground and broke into pieces. Varsha and I looked at each other. We both had no idea what to do with the exploded watermelon.

"Let's take the bigger pieces". The idea struck my head as we gathered the bigger pieces hurriedly and ran back to the hostel room before we were caught red handed by the security guard. We ran and ran and ran. Breathless, we finally reached our room.

"Oh my God!" Varsha saw the watermelon pieces in her hands and laughed.

"It was fun naa". I took the first bite. It was really sweet.

"Your boyfriend is either totally mad or loves you a lot. Or maybe both". She too bit into the watermelon, laughing.

Twenty-One

The morning bell at five shook us out of the slumber we were in. All the three drunkards and I had had a great sleep. The beer had shown its effect. Ginni was awake before everyone else and as I opened my sleepy eyes, I saw her standing in front of the mirror with a face pack all over her face.

"Do you sleep at night? Or do you keep applying face-packs all night long?", I asked in a sleepy voice. I was actually amazed to see her dedication towards her applying face packs as a part of the morning routine.

"Haha. Good Morning," she tried to speak and laugh without contracting face muscles a lot.

"Good morning," I replied and covered my face with the quilt. I was in no mood to go for morning tea. I just wanted to catch up on some extra minutes of sleep. That beer was still on a roll.

Soon, we had assembled on the ground. We were given our equipment for climbing. Rucksack, snow boots, ice-axe, carabiner, descender, mittens, sleeping bag, mat, feather jacket, windcheaters, trousers, water bottle, helmet, crampons (to attach to the snow boots for better grip while climbing on ice), jumar (to fix the movement of the climber on the rope which helps to avoid the fall while climbing). They also demonstrated the use of this equipment. Some of these were to be used in the climbing exercises while the others were to be used during the glacier training. We had to proceed towards the wall for an artificial wall climbing exercise.

"Good Morning everyone. My name is Jagdeep, Jagdeep Singh".

While Rajeev sir was given the charge for the PT and other exercises, Jagdeep Sir was going to be our trainer for the climbing and other related activities.

"I hope you all are ready for the day and have come with the equipments that you were told to bring". He smiled softly. "Coming to the rock climbing, it will be done in five phases and the toughness of the climb will increase with each phase. We will also have two rappelling sessions. Rappelling means coming down from the rock front with the help of a rope and other equipment. You will be told about it in detail later in the classes. I will also take your theory classes for an hour in the evening, so you get to know all the aspects of mountaineering and climbing. Any questions?"

Everyone shook their heads and he kept on teaching. The first phase was of artificial wall climbing. He was strong on words, had a soft smile and was easy on eyes. Pretty much a good trainer. Everyone was holding on to his every word, while my eyes were, again and again, wandering in Vedant's direction.

"This is going to be a team exercise. The height to which individual members of a team would reach will add up to its total score today. You have four hours for practice. The competition will be in the afternoon. You can all wear your harnesses and practice turn-wise. When one member of the team will climb, the other one will hold the rope and belay. Belaying means exerting tension on a climbing rope so that a falling climber does not fall abruptly and is not hurt. Belaying helps the climber to come down from the wall or rock slowly. So, the person who belays needs to be very attentive all the time. If the climber falls at any time while climbing, he will hang in the air because of the rope tied to his harness and the one who belays, will help him come down by releasing the rope slowly. But he needs to be very alert and hold the rope tight to avoid any jerks to the climbers. If he accidently falls without informing, the others must help him in a safe landing. Got it?"

We all were nodding while Jagdeep sir gave us all the important tips for climbing. Then, two climbers from the institute climbed the wall and showed us some important techniques and things to be kept in mind. The demonstration was really exhilarating. Then we started to climb turn wise.

"I can already feel the fire of this competition. Everyone is trying to be near the wall and get more chances to climb to perform better," Aryan suddenly came near me and spoke behind me. "The competition among the team had already started to be felt. Don't you think?"

"Yes. Everyone seems so excited for this course". I could feel the competition in my veins as well.

"Let's do it then. We have to prove that our team is the best". He extended his hand for a high five which I returned. These kinds of things really boost a team feeling.

"Yes. Let's plan out things for our team. It's a team effort after all. Since, I have done it earlier too, I want to share some tips with you too". Vedant walked to us but kept a safe distance from me. Abhishek and Sujoy also joined.

We all sat down and chalked out a plan to perform well as a team. The turns to go for climbing were decided and also who was going to belay during whose climbing was decided. The wall climbing seemed tough to me. I had already hurt my hands and knees. While Aryan, Abhishek and Vedant were doing well in climbing, Sujoy and I were still struggling with it.

Soon it was my turn to climb again. Vedant had been observing me, the way I was struggling with climbing.

"Taara, you need to accept the wall. Do not move away from it. Hug it, accept it and it will accept you. If you will move away from it, you will put unnecessary pressure on your arm muscles and it will ultimately affect your balance and grip on the holds". Vedant came closer and whispered, "Do not take me otherwise. I am just telling you this as you are also part of my team".

It seemed that he wanted to clarify that he is not doing this because of our past relationship.

"Okay. Thanks. I will keep this in mind. Where did you do this before?" I could not hold back my curiosity.

"I have taken the basic course training earlier in Arunachal Pradesh last year". He was happy to provide the information.

"Hmm, thanks for the advice. I hope it helps. I have already hurt my knee badly". As I said that my hand automatically massaged my knee a bit. He smiled. I felt self-conscious and proceeded towards the wall to climb.

After reaching the wall, I took two deep breaths to clear the head. As I looked back, I saw that Vedant had taken charge of the rope. He smiled and showed a thumbs up sign to indicate that he was ready.

I performed better this time. The tips that were given by Vedant actually worked. I balanced well on the wall and the grips were also better. In two or three more practices, I started to understand the basic technique of weight balancing and gripping while climbing.

'He is a changed person or is he just pretending to be like this... calm and composed?' I was wondering if he was the same guy whom I had met and fallen in love with. The one who used to be the impatient college brat.

"It was fun, yaar," Kritika cleared something off her plate with the napkin as we waited for our turn in the mess food queue for the lunch. She was one of those participants who had climbed till the top of the wall on the first day itself. She was an athlete and had better stamina which reflected in her performance.

"Yes, and you did so well". I was really in awe of her.

"But what happened to you. Why did you try only once?" Ginni was blowing air on her renewed nail paint.

"Yaar, I think this is not meant for me. See I scratched my hand in the first attempt itself and my nail is also broken". Ginni showed her nail to us.

"Come on, yaar. We all are hurt a little bit. You should have tried more," Kritika interrupted her. She was booming with happiness because of her excellent performance on the very first day.

"I do not know that but right now I am feeling so hungry. Let's move faster. See people are just entering the queue without their turn". We laughed at her innocence but moved fast. The exercise had made us really hungry.

"You still do not know Ginni's priorities?", Neeti asked Kritika in a sarcastic tone as Ginni proceeded faster in the queue leaving the three of us behind.

"Come on, I am worried about her rope."

."Yeah, I know. She is in my team. Her priorities are going to affect our team performance". We all laughed together.

Twenty-Two

My grades suffered. The late night chats and talks were reflecting on my studies. I was mostly sleep deprived and was unable to concentrate on studies. I had started bunking classes to be with Vedant. From the topper of the class, I had gone down to being an average student. My parents were called up by the college dean and informed about this.

"We have great expectations from her. She is one of the brightest students of our college. But her recent performance in the examinations is very disappointing. Is her health well?" Dean sir was definitely going to tell everything to them.

"Sir, I myself am very surprised with her performance this time. I will talk to her". My mom looked just as worried.

I was called home. It was something that I never wanted to face. I had always made my parents proud. This was the first time that they were feeling ashamed because of me. I was feeling the guilt of hiding things from my parents. Though they did not say much about my low grades but their silence was enough to jitter me from within and make me realize that I was doing something wrong.

'This has to stop. This relationship has to be over. I cannot let my parents down like this'. I was having this thought repeatedly.

I had told Vedant not to call me till I was home. We did not talk for a week. It gave me time to think about the way to end this relationship. I returned to the college the next week and I tried to ignore Vedant. He tried to talk to me but whenever he came near to talk, I changed my way.

The phone was ringing continuously in the classroom.

"You should talk to him once before parting ways with him," Varsha said

"Hmm. I think you are right."

I got up from my classroom and went out towards Vedant's class. He was standing outside with a group of friends. He saw me coming towards him and came towards me.

"What happened, Taara? Why you are not talking to me?"

I was silent.

"What happened? Tell me. Is everything okay?" He was now holding my hand.

"Hmm. Vedant, I wanted to tell you something."

"Tell me. What is it?"

"I wanted to tell you that my parents have fixed my marriage and I have got engaged". I lied as I moved my hand back from his hand. "This relationship has to stop here".

"What? You are too young to get married and.... You... you are joking. Right?"

"No Vedant, I am not joking."

"How can you marry someone else?", he said still trying to believe what I had told him.

"I think whatever parents decide is best for us. I have accepted it."

"But... so suddenly... this... why? I mean... why?" He was trying to figure out what to say.

"I am sorry, Vedant". I was looking at the other side. I did not want to give him time to look into my eyes and realize that I was lying. I did not want him to make me tell the truth as well. I took his hand and slipped the mobile phone, that he had gifted me, into his hand. "Please do not call me".

He did not say a word and stood there, shattered, as I moved away from him.

Twenty-Three

In my rope, as I tried to avoid Vedant, I started talking more with Aryan. We had become good friends. It helped me to stay away from Vedant as I knew Vedant would never want me to talk to other guys. I could feel him getting uncomfortable when I talked to Aryan. He would walk away the moment Aryan and I started talking. Though, for me, Aryan was a good friend and he was also unknowingly helping me to stay away from Vedant. But on some level, I also felt that I was using him.

"Planning, conservation of energy and balancing. These are the major techniques to be kept in mind while mountain climbing". Jagdeep sir had started his theory class. All of us were sitting in the auditorium in the evening. These classes used to be sleepy sometimes, and by sometimes, I mean all the time. As we were already tired after the day's mountaineering practice, it made us droopy.

"Technique and fitness both are equally important for good mountaineering. Both of these need to be balanced properly if you want to be a good mountaineer. You need to understand where and when to use which technique. Techniques need to be changed as per the soil and land conditions. It's your intelligence and experience at this time which helps you decide how to climb on a rocky, loose or grassy soil. You will gradually understand it with experience and learn to use appropriate techniques when it is risky and you are more prone to accidents".

"Sir, does it mean that weather conditions, the condition of the soil, our health and physical strength all have to be focused?" Aryan wasn't much sleepy I feel. Aryan's question had brought me back from my half sleepy state and I saw Vedant looking at me and smiling mischievously.

'Did he see me having the nap?' I was a bit embarrassed and all I could do was to smile back at him to hide my embarrassment.

"Yes, absolutely and never forget that the harness is your friend. It is going to come to your rescue at many times when you lose this balance". Jagdeep sir answered Aryan's question but his eyes came to me quite often.

'Shit. He knew too.'

"How can this guy Aryan remain so attentive in the class after all day's physical work?" Kritika who was sitting beside me could not help commenting.

"I think his mom gave him Chawanprash during his childhood," I replied sarcastically.

"These days you and Aryan are getting close. Aren't you?" Kritika winked.

"No, he is just a friend yaar. Do not jump to conclusions. Okay?"

"Okay okay, irritable grizzly. I was just guessing. Otherwise, he is not a bad choice. Looks are also not bad. Not as good as Vedant here, but..."

"Yeah. You can get into a relationship with him if you are interested. For me, he is just a friend," I replied, a bit irritated. I could not understand the reason for my irritation. Or maybe I know I felt guilty for using him.

"And Vedant…"

“Taara and Kritika. Please do not talk in the class. It disturbs the class,” Jagdeep sir, thankfully, interrupted our talk and we nodded in agreement, assuring to take care in the future.

“So, every expedition is on a track unknown to you which gives you the challenge to use your knowledge and save yourself from danger. No one ever becomes an expert in mountaineering. You are an expert till the time you are able to balance your techniques and be fit, physically and mentally. Mountains are your best friends but also the worst enemies. When they kill, they kill mercilessly. So, never lose the focus and never be overconfident. In most of the cases, it’s the overconfidence which leads to the major accidents,” he kept on telling the golden rules of mountaineering.

“We will start the glacier training next week. Tomorrow, we are going to have a rock climbing competition. All of you should be ready as per the schedule and be ready mentally as well. This training will become tougher day by day from now on,” Jagdeep sir informed and the class ended.

Mr Jagdeep was right. The difficulty level increased in climbing as we proceeded to the next phase. It had started with the wall climbing to rock climbing. The individual competition was going to be at the last phase rock.

The day had come and we were introduced to the rock to be climbed. The competition was to start in some time and everyone was getting ready. This rock was particularly difficult to climb as it had many *Pinch Holds* which are hard to grip on and involve a lot of strength of shoulder muscles.

“Wow. This is difficult,” Vedant exclaimed.

“Haha. When you said wow, I thought it’s easier for you”. Aryan laughed.

“That’s how I express. I am different you know”. I could not help but smile at Vedant’s overconfidence.

"Dude, we still have to perform. Do not be overconfident," I told Vedant. I did not want his performance to suffer because of his overconfidence.

"Don't worry, I will take care," he replied lovingly, coming closer to me. He could sense that I still cared for him. Maybe others can too.

"No, I just mean that the institute coaches are reminding us, again and again, to not be overconfident," I tried giving the explanation which was not even needed. Vedant smiled mischievously and I left from there, embarrassed at my own behaviour.

Jagdeep sir was standing at the top of the rock, encouraging everyone. "You can do it Taara!" He was shouting.

I was losing my grip over the hand-hold. I had climbed half of the rock and was left with no strength to climb on. The difficulty level of rock was increasing as I moved further.

"I cannot do it, sir. My hands are aching," I replied loudly.

"You can. Just try a bit more. Use techniques along with the strength". He motivated me again.

I gathered my confidence and remembered the techniques that were taught to us. I implemented a few and was able to climb further.

Everyone rejoiced as I climbed and hooted to encourage me.

I could hear Vedant shouting, "Taara, you are the best. Nothing is impossible for you. Just do it."

As I heard him, I felt the sudden urge to turn back and see him shouting my name. I left the hand hold that I was gripping on to. His motivating words had a different effect on me. As I left the rock, I descended slowly down, my eyes looking at Vedant. He had a confused expression as if asking why I had left the hold when it was in my grip. I loved to see that expression. I knew that I had intentionally lost this competition, but I had realized that I was still in love with him. I still loved him idiotically and his quizzical eyes kept boring into mine.

Twenty-Four

I had not seen Vedant for a week now. It had been two months since we stopped talking. But before this, I could see him in college every two or three days. Even a glimpse of him was still important to me.

I do not understand why love makes us so stupid. Why the feelings that are connected to the heart kill the efficacy of the mind? Why is suppressing one's feelings considered wise and expressing them is considered stupidity?

I was an expert at being wise in most situations before I met Vedant. He introduced me to myself and more importantly, the person inside me who was not wise, who knew to express and who was free. As I got away from him, I was getting back to my wise-self and had started missing the stupid self who was again going away from me slowly. It seemed I had not lost him but myself too.

'Where is Vedant since so many days? Has he gone home?' I could not resist thinking about him again and again. It was me who had told him to be away but his disappearance suddenly was bothering me to my core.

I thought about calling him. But I had not kept his number with me.

‘Why did not I keep his number? I am so stupid’. I was cursing myself. It had been ten days and I had not seen or heard about him. I was tossing in my bed and could not sleep.

“Hi”. I had gone to meet Sarvesh to enquire about him.

“Hi”. He had a strange annoyed expression in his eyes.

“Hmmmm, where is Vedant? Is he not coming to college?”

“No. You do not know about it?” His annoyed expressions turned into surprise.

“No. What happened?”

“I guess the whole college knows about it and that’s why I thought… Well, out of everyone, you do not… know it… because of whom it has happened,” he said with an angry mockish tone.

“What… because of me? What has happened?”

“Vedant is totally shattered after you left him. He had been drinking heavily and does not talk to anyone. We were trying hard to get him back to normal. Around ten days back, he was drunk and he rammed his bike into the road divider. He is badly hurt. He has been hospitalized. He loves you so much. How could you leave him? How could you do this to him?”

“Oh!” My head was spinning. “What have I done? All this happened because of me”.

“Do not worry. He is stable now. He had hurt his head and his arm is fractured. He will be discharged from hospital in another two or three days.”

“I have to meet him.”

“I don’t think you should.”

“Please.”

I took the hospital address and went to meet Vedant that very moment. I could not control my tears the whole way to the hospital.

Vedant was lying on the hospital bed, his eyes closed. His forehead was covered with bandages and right arm had been plastered. I went close to him, dragged a stool to his bed and took his left hand into mine. Tears rolled down my eyes as I kept staring at his hand.

"I am fine. Why are you weeping?" He had woken up and was looking at me.

"I am sorry Vedant. It all happened because of me". I was weeping uncontrollably.

"Please do not cry. You do not have to feel guilty. It is because of my bad habits. You should not blame yourself for this".

"No, I should be blamed Vedant as I lied to you and broke your heart. I hurt the person who loves me so much".

"Lie…. What lie?" He tried getting up. I softly pushed him back to his lying position.

"I am not getting married, Vedant. I had lied to you so that you go away from me".

"But why?"

"Vedant, my parents have some expectations from me. I was a bright student before I met you but then, I could not concentrate on my studies after falling in love with you. I wanted to go away from you and not ditch my parents". I let it all go in one breath and cried more.

He had a happy expression on his face as if he heard nothing what I told him after he heard that I wasn't getting married. As if nothing else mattered.

"What?", I asked as he continued to stare at me lovingly.

“Nothing. You continue”.

“What continue? How will you write your exams now? You have hurt your right arm”. I changed the topic. If he was angry, I could have taken it. But he was not and that was giving me a guilt trip.

“Don’t worry. I will get the exam papers leaked and written by a friend”.

“Shut up. I am serious”. I was laughing. It felt so normal.

“Really! I am serious. And you do not have to worry about your grades too. I will get exam papers for you too. Trust me, I can do that. I have contacts”.

I laughed again.

“And now can you concentrate on studies after going away from me?” His eyes were accusing now.

“Umm. No, I felt like I died”.

“Then be with me. This is how it is meant to be. We will talk only at night and weekends. You can concentrate on studies. I will not disturb you,” he said with a child-like convincing tone.

I could not help but smile.

“Come here”. He opened his non fractured arm for a hug and I gladly took it. He wiped my tears with his hand. I could not believe that a person with a broken head and arm could still care about my tears. I was dying inside by his love and gentleness. He bent forward in the hug and hugged me even more tightly. Then, he mildly withdrew as his face came nearer to mine. We had hugged each other earlier too but this time it was different. His eyes were fireballs as he bent, closer into my face and I closed my eyes. He kissed me… gently, as if I’d break. It was our first kiss. I wanted to melt in the arms of this man who loved me so much. He kissed me gently again and we hugged again.

“Thank God! You are not getting married”. He whispered in my ears as I felt the tickle.

Twenty-Five

The basic course training of fifteen days at the institute was over. While Abhishek from our rope had to leave the course in middle for some urgent work assignment, my performance was also only average. But Kritika, Vedant, Aryan and six other mountaineers from the other ropes were giving each other a tough fight for the top slot and the highest grades in the course.

Today, we had to proceed to the base camp for the next ten days where we had to undergo advanced course of glacier training. The glacier trekking and climbing was going to decide the ranking team wise as well as the individual grades.

We had packed our rucksacks and soon we were ready to leave the institute at six in the morning. The SUVs were waiting for us. We had to travel a part of the way to the base camp on roads and the rest of the way would be covered by trekking.

As we gained height, the air became cooler. After an hour, SUVs dropped us at a high altitude mountain where we ate our packed breakfast which we had brought with us from the mess. The lunch was planned at the base-camp.

We started trekking towards the base-camp after the breakfast. It was around ten kilometres of trek to the base camp. The route was very interesting as it had various types of trails, rocky, sandy, soily, grassy, narrow and steep. We could see why the course developers had selected this route. Here we will be getting experience of all kinds of trails.

"The route will help you get insight of the basics of mountaineering". That were exactly Rajeev sir's words from the instructions that he had given in the morning before leaving the institute. Both Mr. Rajeev and Mr. Jagdeep were accompanying us in the trek to the base camp and were giving necessary instructions from time to time.

"Stop only when the whole group stops. Do not separate yourself from the group. If anyone feels any difficulty or uneasiness, he or she should inform me. But do not isolate yourself from the group," Rajeev sir reminded us yet again. It is difficult to be responsible for others. In trekking, any kind of irresponsibility can lead to very bad outcomes.

I, Kritika and Aryan were walking together. The cold air was grazing my cheeks and just under ten minutes, it started to feel numb. But a deep enthralling happiness was engulfing me. It was a feeling like a cold freezing hand of a loved one on the cheeks.

Neeti and Ginni were walking in the end. Ginni was finding it very difficult to trek and was expressing her wish to go back home after almost every fourth step that she took. Neeti was trying to motivate her to move on. We were enjoying the fun.

In these fifteen days, Neeti and Ginni had become very good friends. They were enjoying this course more than anyone else. Sometimes finding a great friend supersedes every other situation in life. I could see that happening with both of them.

"You should not use ear-phones while trekking," Jagdeep sir told Kritika as she was listening to songs.

"But why, sir?"

"How are you going to hear the sounds around you while trekking if you have earphones plugged into your ears? Your team member maybe calling you for help or a vehicle maybe honking its horn or while walking through jungle, you will need to be alert to various sounds of animals. How will you understand your surroundings if you will close one such important sense of your body?", he explained.

"He has a point". Aryan looked at Mr. Jagdeep with wide eyes.

"Sir, actually I was not listening to songs. I have just plugged in earphones to save my ears from Aryan's non-stop talks," Kritika teased him.

"Okay. Then it is fine". Jagdeep sir could not help but smile at Kritika's joke.

"You and your PJs". I started laughing loudly.

"Such jokes are not PJs, Taara. These are DPJs. Kritika specials". Aryan was mischievously looking at us.

"DPJ? What is that?" Kritika looked with quizzical eyes.

"Deadly Poor Joke". Aryan and I had a hearty laugh. Kritika joined in too.

Vedant who was walking ahead of us, turned back to look at us. He was among the ones who walked really fast even on mountains.

"He must be wondering why we have suddenly gone mad," I whispered to Kritika.

"Yeah. and you are enjoying this? Aren't you?", She asked with a very teasing tone.

"Enjoying what? I don't know what you are talking about".

"Do not be so innocent. You are trying to tease him. Aren't you?" Kritika winked.

"Not exactly". I smiled and looked ahead at Vedant. He had already glanced twice again after that.

Twenty-Six

Vedant and I had been together for a year now. As I could feel his love growing for me with every passing day, I could also feel myself caged in an invisible prison of his possessiveness. The relationship was becoming more and more about him. He did not like me being close to any of my friends and most of my time was spent with Vedant. I was not doing great in studies but I had compromised with that as I always chose Vedant over everything else.

The day to day quarrels over small and big issues were becoming routine now. I always tried to avoid the conflict but somehow things were not coming back on track.

"Hey I have made a fantastic plan for your birthday". He sounded really excited. My birthday was in the coming week.

"Oh and you won't be telling me about it, right? It would be a surprise, isn't it?" He knew that I liked surprises on special occasions like this.

"No surprises this time. It will be a planned birthday. Though, you may get some surprises after reaching there". He was getting more and more excited.

"After reaching where?"

"The place where we are going this weekend."

"What are you saying? Care to tell me clearly?"

"We are going to Nainital for your birthday. We will stay there for your birthday plus another day and celebrate there. I have talked to a friend who has his five-star hotel there."

"But Vedant how can we go to Nainital? It is too far".

"Where do you want to go then?" Vedant's voice went a notch lower.

"Any one day trip Vedant like we went last time to that hill-station. It was such a nice trip, yaar. You know naa, I cannot stay out at night". I was still not okay with lying to my parents about staying with a guy.

"Why? What is the issue with that? I told you last time too that I will manage your home phone calls. Then what is the problem now?" He was getting annoyed at my refusal to go out. His tone was angry suddenly.

"It's not about the phone calls, Vedant."

"Then what is it about? You do not trust me or what?"

"Why are you taking things otherwise? You know I love you and I trust you so much. It's just that I have never stayed out without informing my parents and I cannot do it now too. I will feel guilty if I will do that".

"Oh come on. Don't you feel guilty of hiding our affair from them? Don't you?"

"Yes. Thanks for reminding me".

"So you can lie about this as well."

"Being in a relationship and staying out at night are two different things."

"Wow. I think I am incapable of understanding your hi-fi logic about feeling guilty. Please explain how it is different". I could see anger in his eyes rising every second.

"I cannot explain it to you because you do not want to understand. You are just worried about your own views and you do not care what I am comfortable with and what I am not."

"What do you want me to understand? You are just a hypocrite". His anger was right there with us, back in our relationship.

"Like always you have decided the plan for us on your own and now you cannot accept a change in the plan. You can't accept what I feel".

"Yes, I made the plan and it was for your birthday. You talk about surprises. What's the use of it if you'll never get to do anything new? But you do not care about my wishes and are behaving selfishly. You don't care about me, Taara. My emotions do not matter to you. I really wanted to go out with you and you want to spoil everything".

"I am not saying that I won't go out with you. I just cannot stay out at night. Try and understand, Vedant," I tried to explain again.

"Oh forget it. Trying to make you understand is useless. I will cancel the trip. Happy?" He angrily stomped away.

"Vedant... Vedant..". I called him but in vain.

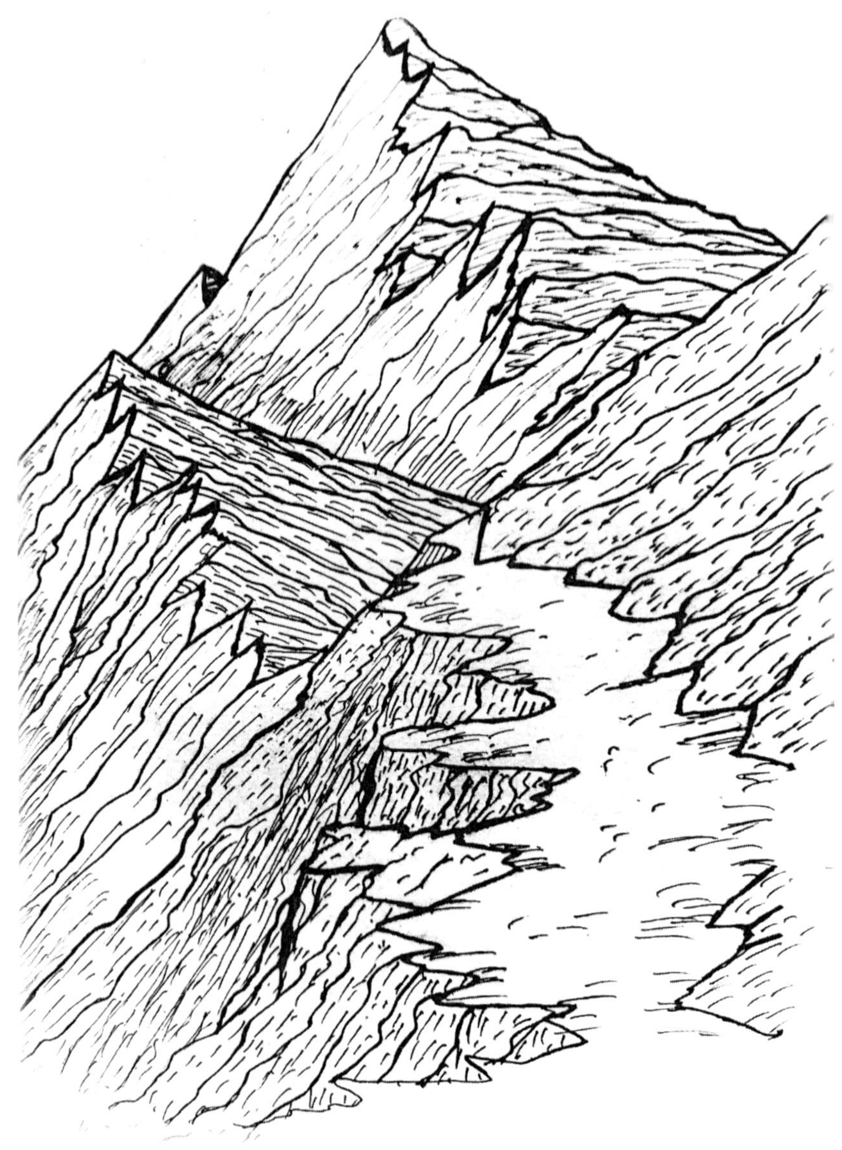

Twenty-Seven

We reached the base camp which was at a height of fourteen thousand feet. We caught the first glimpse of the tents that were lined and anchored in the grassland, partially covered with fresh snow. Here, it snowed everyday which also melted on sunrise side by side. In the middle of this green valley surrounded by the snowclad mountains from all sides, the tents looked mesmerizing. I had not visited such a beautiful and cold place in my life. The cold breeze was freezing us.

Mountains teach us not to give up. They are also the symbol of climbing heights in life and the journey may have phases where we need to take a break. But this does not mean we should give up before reaching our destiny. Destiny unfolds with time and we need to move on at our own pace.

Sometimes we feel the path is very tiring and steep. It makes us feel that we cannot reach our destiny. At such moments, we need to gather our courage and get up again to walk further. Many times, people just give up trying when they are so close to their destiny and they never realize this.

Everyone had reached the base camp. Some earlier, while some took their own time.

"Thank God, we have finally reached," Ginni said catching her breath, "I was sure I was going back".

“Wow. This is so beautiful, yaar, and wait..... we are going to stay in tents? Yay,” Neeti exclaimed her surprise and joy at the first view of the base camp. Kritika and I were standing near the edge of the camp, waiting for them.

All four of us roommates were standing together, rejoicing and having the view of the base camp.

‘Why is he coming here?’ I had a quick thought as I saw Vedant coming towards me. It seemed that he wanted to talk to me about something. I moved a bit away from my roommates and went towards Vedant. I don’t know why, but I still seemed to orient myself according to him. I knew I loved him still and this vacation was going to be a beautiful journey of mine. But somehow, Vedant was becoming an integral part of this journey.

“Congrats. you are among the first ones to reach the base camp. Your performance is really improving,” he said, initiating the talk.

“Thanks”. I didn’t know why my tongue felt stuck to all the bases of my body and refused to move enough to talk.

“You had come to tell me this?”, I said after a pause, breaking the silence.

“No. I mean I wanted to say ‘hi’ too. Hmmm, actually I wanted to say… I wanted to talk to you”. He paused and looked hopefully towards me.

“What? Is everything okay?” I could feel nervousness in his voice.

“Nothing. Just capture your tent, else you will get only the ones left out in the end,” he said that with a lot of effort. It seemed as he deliberately deviated from the topic.

“Huh? Oh, okay. Yeah, we are going to do that. Thanks”.

He turned around, walking away.

"You never remembered me in all these years?" He suddenly turned back to me again and asked. Like a spell, he broke after a lot of effort.

I was spellbound, not knowing what to say.

"I do not know about you. But I could never forget you. I kept wishing to meet you once more in life just to tell you that there is no one like you in the whole world," he said emotionally in one go.

"I… I do not know what to say… Vedant… Actually…". I tried to find words to say.

"Taara, I do not want to force you to love me. But I want to tell you how I still feel about you before this course ends. It may be my last chance to tell you what I think about... telling you that I missed you every single day since you left. We may or may not meet after this course… I still miss you, Taara". He said looking into my eyes searching for an answer.

"Vedant… Right now, I do not know what I want…"

"It's okay. I just wanted to tell you my feelings. Do not worry. You do not have to say anything". He again paused. Then he suddenly changed the topic and made an innocent face with a smile. "Okay. Now stop making such a serious face. Go and capture your tent. Else, you will blame me for wasting your time and not getting a good tent".

"Okay". That was all I could manage to say. I could see the love in his eyes but did not know how to respond to his love. I had tough time recovering from it. Maybe I never recovered, never. He bid goodbye and went back.

I went towards my roommates who were still standing together and gossiping.

"What happened?", Kritika asked.

"Nothing as such. Just a casual talk", I replied.

"Ahem ahem. Casual talks of love you mean?", Ginni teased.

I could not help but smile as they all enjoyed teasing me.

Twenty-Eight

Vedant made issues of the things that seemed petty to me. I kept trying to find space to breathe and be the person that I was. But Vedant could not stand this at all.

Mind is a jumbled mess sometimes, especially when you are in love. In love, even when you know what is wrong in your relationship, you still want it to work out somehow. But we forget that nothing works out on its own. We cling on to the person without understanding that it will cause more harm to us. Sometimes it is too hard to leave, too hard to let go until it is the only option left.

Most of us try to do our best, just to work on our relationships. This was happening with me too. I was losing myself in this relationship but still I was too much in love to let it go. It was the anxiety of losing my dream to excel in my field of study, ditching my parents who had dreams to see their daughter shine in her career. I was compromising everything and was becoming the person that Vedant wanted me to become.

However, what pinched me the most was Vedant's behaviour when he was drunk. Vedant was a different person after he was drunk. The things he said in that state and which he tend to forget the next day became very hurtful for me. I could not forget things as easily as he could. I had asked him to quit drinking but he never took it seriously and ignored my concern. He did not understand that I could not take things as lightly as he did.

Varsha was no longer a close friend. We were still roommates but a weird kind of coldness had surfaced in our friendship. I hid many things from her as Vedant did not like our matters and chats to be discussed with anyone else. This was something very unusual for two friends who used to share everything earlier. Varsha had eventually realized the change in my behaviour and she stopped talking much to me. I could feel that I had hurt her though she never said anything. She now had a new group of friends in the class. Megha, Siddharth and Varsha were seen mostly together during college hours. I could feel her absence and I felt it more as I saw her getting close to her other friends. I felt like I was getting replaced in her life and I was eventually losing a dear friend. It seemed as if Taara was actually losing her Sitaara.

"Hey! What is this stupid card doing on my desk?", Varsha said, when she saw a 'sorry card' lying on her study table.

I had decided that I could not lose my other relationships like this. I wanted to be with my friends too. I had made a sorry card for Varsha with a girl cartoon holding her ears and saying 'Sorry Varsha. You are my best friend. Please Forgive Me. My Sitaara.'

"I am sorry yaar," I said getting up from my bed and moving towards Varsha.

"I can understand. I am sorry too". She hugged me.

No more complains and Taara Sitaara were back again, best buddies, just like earlier. We talked for God knows how many hours. I told her everything that I had been holding on to since so many months and she told me hers too.

"Ahhhhhh....". I took a deep breath of relief.

"What happened?"

"Nothing. I feel free. Free from the stomach ache". I smiled. She laughed out loud.

"Hey Taara, where are you?" I had got a call from Vedant. I had come outside the classroom to talk.

"Hi Vedant, I am in college".

"Come outside in the ground area after your class. I want to meet you".

"Vedant, I have another class after this one".

"A class in the lunch time?"

"Yes. An extra class". I lied to him. Siddharth was giving us a treat at a nearby restaurant. I, Varsha, Megha and Siddharth were going to have lunch together. Though Vedant wouldn't have liked it, I really wanted to be a part of this group. I had been feeling so much friends deprived in the last few months.

"Arey come naa, yaar. You can miss this class, can't you?"

"Sorry Vedant. This class is important. Okay? Bye. I need to go now. See you in the evening," I said disconnecting the call.

I was feeling something in the pit of my stomach, but ignoring it for now as it seemed like the best option.

Twenty-Nine

There was no water in the base camp. We had to use tissues and wet wipes for day to day things. The purpose of staying here was to make us all aware of the hardships that we would face while going on various mountain expeditions.

"Wow. Chana Poori. Halwa. Oh my God! I saw it in my dream last night and see it's here," Aryan exclaimed his happiness on seeing the breakfast. We all had made a queue as the breakfast was being served.

"The breakfast is so yummy. Eating fried things in the cold have their own charm". Ginni was on her second helping already.

"You have to walk a lot today. So, have a heavy breakfast. But not too much because that will make walking really heavy," Rajeev Sir said, as he overheard Aryan and Ginni.

"Where are we going today?" Aryan didn't care about looking at anyone but his poori chana.

"We are going for a height gain trek to get you all acclimatized to the height and the difficult treks of the glaciers. We will start in sometime and will come back by the evening. Your lunch will also be packed to have it on the way"

We all had started our day's journey with rucksacks on our back. We were given all the important instructions and were told about the day's plan in detail. The path was fine till the time it was green. As the greenery ended, the rocky trek started which was very difficult to walk on and needed a lot of attention. It was getting more and more difficult as we gained more height. Oxygen levels were getting lower. There was less vegetation in the area and a peculiar fragrance of plants was coming which was causing a headache.

All were segregated. Everyone was walking at their own pace. I was mostly walking alone. Even though I was meeting one friend or the other on the way, I actually wanted to walk alone at my own pace. The trek was getting tougher and breathlessness was increasing.

I saw Vedant sitting at a stone, resting and catching hold of his breath.

"Tired?", I asked the stupid question to start the conversation.

"A bit," he said getting up and started walking with me.

"This trek is so difficult, yaar. I am already tired and it's only half way now". I felt like sharing more. More he replied; more we could talk.

"Yes it's a difficult one. But this will help them to identify the real climbers for their expeditions in future, na?" He was looking deep in my eyes.

"You are right but I am already so tired and breathless. Every now and then, I feel the need to stop and take rest". I didn't blink either.

"Okay. Let's stop for some time and take rest". He smiled and I felt a blush rising.

He took out some dry fruits from his pocket and gave me to eat. I gave him my chocolate.

"You still eat this chocolate," his voice rose in exclamation, as he instantly recognized the brand that I used to eat in college as well.

"Yes. Nothing has changed," I said blushing, as if I gave him a hint that I still loved him. I knew I did. Maybe so should he.

We sat silently on a large tree trunk for some time.

"Let's make a plan".

"What kind of plan?"

"A plan to do this trek because it looks pretty difficult."

"Okay and what is the plan?"

"We will not stop before walking at least fifty steps. Only after taking fifty steps further, we can take rest. What do you say?"

"It sounds like a good plan. We can definitely try".

We walked the steps together, counting them and taking rest every now and then. Vedant motivated me whenever I felt like giving up.

"Come on. We are about to reach now. You cannot give up now. Come".

"You are saying this for the last half an hour. But we have not reached yet. You are fooling me". I started complaining like a child.

"Arey, this time we are actually about to reach. Come, have a view from here".

I went near him. We could see snow now. The path ahead of us had snow on the sides. The snow spots had started to appear in the path. As we proceeded further, the snow increased on the path.

"Hey! We have almost reached," I expressed my happiness, as I could see some of our friends now.

"Yes, we were destined to reach together," Vedant said, smiling. This time he was holding my hand lightly in his.

There was a sense of assurance that we felt while trekking a path which is known to be travelled by trekkers. It makes it feel safe. While if we trek on the same path without knowing that it is used by people, we will feel scared or not so safe. The path is same. We are same. But the assurance of the path being known has gone away.

Similar are the situations in our life. The path being followed by others seems known and easier to us because we have seen someone live it. The paths which are different appear difficult. At such moments, we need to gather the courage to choose the paths to our destiny and understand that everyone must travel their life journey alone. The fear of the unknown is the biggest obstacle to the freedom of soul. We need to overcome this to live the life which truly brings us happiness.

We had our lunch there. Chicken rice felt like the tastiest dish in the world, after all the hard work. Soon, we started our journey back to the base camp. It was a downward trek now mostly, so it was easier and less tiring. Kritika, I and Aryan were together this time.

"Where is Ginni?" I asked as I could find only Kritika and Neeti there.

"She went back on the halfway. Someone was saying that she is not well".

"Oh, I hope she is fine". I was so busy with Vedant, I never paid attention to my friend.

It started to snow in sometime. The cotton like snowflakes felt beautiful. I was enjoying the walk. Soon, we started having the view of the base camp and a feeling of having reached back home took over everyone. Now, we just wanted to reach the base camp fast and settle down.

Thirty

I knew Vedant did not want me to go to Siddharth's treat and would somehow convince me otherwise. Though I really wanted to go there, I'll rather not go to avoid arguments with him and so, I had lied to him for the extra class. When I told him I won't meet him after class, he insisted that I should meet him in the evening instead.

I wanted to spend time with my friends too as I did earlier before I met Vedant and this seemed like an awesome opportunity. We went to the restaurant and had fun. It was an awesome time out with friends after so long.

In the evening, I called Vedant. I knew he'd want to see me soon. But he did not come to meet me in the evening. I kept waiting for him and calling him continuously. But he didn't pick up. After too many calls, he finally started disconnecting my call and that made me worried.

"Where are you?", I asked worriedly when Vedant finally picked up my call. It was eight in the night and I had been calling for two hours.

"Why are you asking?" His rude tone meant something was wrong.

"What happened? Why are you talking like this? I was waiting for you outside the college but you did not come". I felt like crying.

"Nothing happened. I just do not want to talk to you". He said in a drunken tone.

"Are you drunk?"

"Yes. You have any problem?"

"Enough, Vedant. Why do you have to talk so rudely with me when you are drunk?"

"Wow. You are so innocent".

"What are you saying?"

"You had an extra class, right?"

"Ummm, yeah".

"At the restaurant… How was it?"

I was thunderstruck right at the place I was standing. 'How did he come to know? He isn't guessing. He knows. It would be one of his khabri friends. They work like spies in my life. What the hell?' I had a quick thought.

"I am sorry, Vedant, that I lied to you. It was Siddharth's lunch treat. His brother had gotten married last week. He just wanted to share his happiness. If I would have told you, you would not have wanted me to go. So… I am sorry".

"Why do you have to be sorry? And yeah, Siddharth… yes… You are with him these days in class, na?"

"What? Why are you making it sound like this? You are twisting the things unnecessarily. I, Varsha, Megha and Siddharth, we all are together in class. We all are friends".

"Oh… friends... with a guy? What a joke, Taara?"

"Joke? Vedant... You are taking it wrong. It's not like this".

"Shut up. You think I am a fool". His words were unclear and drowsy and his pitch was very high.

THUD! I heard the sound of something falling and the

call disconnected. I tried calling him again and again but his phone was switched off.

'Has he hurt himself? Should I go to his apartment? Will that be fine? I have never gone to his apartment earlier. But what if he needs help right now? Stupid guy. Why does he drink so much?' There was a brainstorming session going on inside my head as I continuously tried to call him. I didn't want to go to his apartment so late. I had never been there. But I knew where he lived.

"The number you are trying to call is currently switched off". I never hated this lady's recorded voice as much as I did today but it kept repeating the same line, over and over again.

Thirty-One

"Hey what happened to you?" I asked Ginni as I entered her tent.

"Yaar, I was feeling so uncomfortable and had trouble in breathing. Then I started having severe headache so I stopped on the way and informed Jagdeep sir".

"He arranged for you to be sent back to base camp?"

"Yes".

"How are you now?"

"I am fine. But the doctors have told me not to climb. They say it is because of AMS. Acute Mountain Sickness. That thing we studied about in our theory class."

"Oh. Yes, I remember. You had the same symptoms?"

"Yes, almost".

"Hmm. So how will you climb now?"

"Well. The doctor has advised me to be at lower altitudes only so I will stay at the base camp itself for the coming days and then trail back with you guys. Simple".

"Oh no".

"It's okay, yaar. I am not sad at all. I was actually finding it quite tough and wanted to quit somehow. It is good that this happened. Now I will relax here".

"You are too much. I think you should take rest now. I will bring tea for you here only. It is being served outside".

"Yes please. Please send Neeti too if she has reached back".

"Of course. She herself will come running to you the moment she reaches back. You know that," I said and left the tent.

"The thing that you wanted has finally happened?" Neeti said entering the tent, where I and Ginni were having tea.

"What do you mean? I am actually really sick."

"I do not think so. Prove it", Neeti was laughing loudly.

"You cannot be my friend. Are friends like this, Kritika?", Ginni moaned.

"Haha. Stop teasing her, Neeti. She is actually not well," Kritika said, coming to her rescue.

"She has AMS, guys. She also has the symptoms," I told them.

"Really? AMS?", Neeti mischievously replied.

"Yes".

"Oh my God…," Neeti said opening her mouth in astonishment.

"But what the hell is that?", Kritika asked teasing her more.

"If you would have been attentive in your theory classes, you would not be asking this silly question". Ginni was getting more annoyed.

"That was taught only in the theory class, na? Why are you doing it practically then? Getting AMS and all...," Neeti said, laughing more.

Ginni grabbed a pillow lying near and threw it at Neeti. As she missed the target, she threw another pillow at her.

"This patient is getting violent. Please, someone, call the doctor," Neeti said and we all laughed.

Thirty-Two

My heart had won the battle over my mind and I decided to go to Vedant's rented apartment. Since it was very near to my hostel, I hoped I would be able to go there on foot and reach soon. I was worried about him as he was badly drunk and was alone in his apartment. Even his roommate had gone home for some family function.

"Hi," I said as he opened the door.

"Come inside," he said, hiding the surprised expressions in his eyes. He was, in fact, shocked to see me there.

"No, I just wanted to confirm that you are fine. Your phone is switched off and I had been calling it like a maniac".

"Yes. It is broken".

"Oh". I did not say anything else.

'How could anyone break his latest iPhone? It is worse than a heart break,' I thought. It was hard for me to believe this.

"Come inside." He said again.

I went inside. The apartment was a huge one for a student. Vedant was a pampered kid and everything in his apartment shouted that. He had everything from a fridge to an AC in his apartment. These are not common things to have in the college days. But the apartment was in a messy condition.

Clothes, liquor bottles and much more was lying around in his drawing room.

"Come sit here, Taara". He cleared a little space on the couch and pointed me to sit.

We both sat in silence for some time.

"I was worried, Vedant. Why do you have to drink so much? Do you think it's good for you and our relationship?", I asked

"Do not start that again, Taara. Leave all that... wait... you are here for the first time," he said that as he realized that and went inside another room to get something. Maybe his bedroom.

He came back with a packet and sat beside me.

"Why you had to lie to me?"

"Why do you think?"

"Taara..."

"I am sorry, Vedant. I really am. But I miss my friends. I want to be with my friends too sometimes".

"But why? You do not feel good with me?"

"I do. You know it's not that".

"Then why, Taara?"

I remained silent. He was behaving like a kid who wanted to know why his doll has to be shared with his sister. How can you make someone understand why do you want to have a social life with your friends? Why does he think I don't need a life just because I am in a relationship with him? He too has friends. Why does he think I won't need some too?

"You know why I wanted to meet you?" He was trying to make his words clear as he was badly drunk.

"No. Why?"

He took out a jewellery box from the packet and handed it over to me.

"See. What I got for you?"

I opened the box. It was a gold chain with a beautiful heart shaped pendent of Vedant and my picture in it as it was opened. I looked at him in surprise.

"This is for you. I wanted to give it to you. But you spoiled my mood".

"I am sorry Vedant. But, I cannot accept such a costly gift. You know that".

"Will you please listen? This is not just a gift".

"Then what is it?"

"This is my proposal for marriage. Our marriage". He took the gold chain out of the box and held it in both of his hands. I could not say anything. This was very unexpected at this moment when I just came to see if he was hurt. He opened the hook of gold chain.

"My college will be over in next coming months. I will be taking over dad's business and then, I want to get married to you as soon as possible". He started bending towards me with the chain in his hands. He put his arms around my neck to make me wear it and clasped the lock behind it.

"Vedant…" Something was wrong. I wanted to stop him. I tried to stop him but he was not listening. He came closer so his face was near my cheek and his breath was touching my cheeks. The warm breath also brought the smell of liquor to my nose. He hugged me tight. Then, very slowly, his lips touched the nape of my neck and parted as a gush of warm air touched my neck. The same air which was condensed with a lot of alcohol in it.

"Vedant…" I tried to push him back softly.

"What happened? You did not like the chain?"

"No, no. It is beautiful. Vedant, it is not about the chain".

"Then come closer. We are getting married soon. Aren't you happy?" He was kissing my cheek now.

'How could I marry him? I was nothing. I made nothing of myself for my parents. He loves me. And he loves me so much that I feel trapped by him. I can't do this. I can NOT do this. No...'

"Vedant, I am not ready for this".

"Ready for what? Marriage or getting physically closer to me?", he asked trying to hide his anger.

"Both, Vedant".

"What do you mean? Don't you love me?"

"I love you a lot. You know that too. But this is not the right time for... for any of this".

"Don't worry about your studies. You can continue your studies after marriage".

"No. See, you are not getting it. It's not about studies even. I want to make a career. I want to have a job and then get married. Marriage is not in my plans yet. We will talk about it tomorrow. You are drunk right now. We will talk when you are sober. You sleep now". I got up to leave.

"Wait. You can work after marriage also, Taara. Even if you will not work, it will hardly matter. You will never be in dearth of money. You will be my queen," he said as he got up and held my hand again.

"Okay, Vedant. I will think about it. We will talk tomorrow".

"No. You cannot leave like this". He pulled my hand towards him and put his arms around my waist.

"Leave me, Vedant. I want to go now".

"No. I won't. Are you scared that I will leave you?"

"No, Vedant. I am just not prepared for this. I am not READY," I said, struggling to get out of his hold around my waist.

"What rubbish? We have been together for a year now and you are still not prepared. Neither for marriage, nor for getting closer to me. You are not prepared," he said his voice raising. Suddenly his voice turned venomous.

"Leave me, Vedant. It has nothing to do with the year we spent together. We will talk tomorrow," I said sternly.

"Oh! I... now I understand… you want to be close to that Siddharth now. Your new lover, for whom you lied to me". He pushed my hand angrily.

"How can you even think like that? Your thinking is so narrow. He is my friend".

"I very well understand such friendships and I understand girls like you too".

"What did you say?" I was too shocked to comprehend what he said.

"Go to him then". This time Vedant pushed me with all the force he could muster.

I could not handle the push and hit the nearby table. The back of my head hit the table and my elbow hit badly on the ground as I tried to balance myself. My elbow was bleeding and the head was throbbing with pain.

"Oh my God! I am so sorry, Taara. Shit. What did I do?" Vedant came running towards me, realizing what he had done in his drunken state.

"Stop, Vedant. Do not touch me," I said somehow trying to get up. "Thanks for treating me like this. This was important to make me realize how much self-respect I have lost in an attempt to be with you. You couldn't stop at anything in belittling me because I said no to you. Thank you. I am going. And this time, forever, Vedant," I said as I took out the chain from my neck and kept it on the table I was thrown at just now.

"Sorry, Taaraa. Listen...". I didn't. I knew if I stopped now, I will regret it for whole my life.

"Good Bye, Vedant," I said it without even looking at him and slammed the door to his apartment. My eyes were flooded with tears. My head was pounding and ears ringing. My elbow was hurt and I couldn't stop. I had to go. I had to go on.

Thirty-Three

Can you ever become friends again with the person you were once in love with? I had never thought I would again be friends with Vedant. I might have hoped, but I had never thought I would be even meeting him again. The person whom I loved once and the same person whom I was trying to avoid now had again became my friend. He was here and my heart… all the snow on my heart melted like he was the summer I was waiting for. All my efforts to avoid him had been in vain. Maybe I still loved him and I wanted to be close to him. Whenever my mind had this thought, I would console it by thinking that we are just friends. Nothing more than this. But it's not true. I accepted that I still care about him. Even that I still love him. But do I love him enough that I can let go of the past and be with him?

"I am enjoying Vedant's company again. I have always done that in the past too. Last time, I bounded myself to him. But, this time I don't feel like I am bounded anymore. I feel free. He is not that dominant Vedant as he used to be in college days," I told Kritika as we reached the glacier.

"It is too early to judge. You said, he wasn't that possessive Vedant in the early days of your college days as well. But still, I will tell you to follow your heart. The heart never lies. At least that's true in my case". Kritika was contradicting her own sentences.

“We are mostly together these days while treks and the way he motivates me and the love I can see in his eyes. I do not know how to stop myself from falling in love with him again”.

“Do not stop then. That is what I am telling you. Let things happen the way they are bound to happen. Do not resist your destiny. But also keep your eyes wide open.”

“Hmm, I think you are right,” I said, as we got ready for the day.

The last days in the training were getting tougher. Some of the participants of the course had already quit the course. Sujoy was one of them. Only three members were left in our team now: I, Vedant and Aryan.

Today, we were being given the glacier training where we had to climb a big rock, covered with snow.

‘The big mountain that stood tall in front of us felt like it is our ego. The bigger the ego is, the more difficult the journey will be to overcome it, similar to a steep mountain which is so difficult to climb. But I had to overcome my ego and this huge mountain too. To conquer it, I would have to conquer my insides, myself and my inhibitions. That will be an achievement in itself, as big as climbing the mountain itself,’ I thought.

Knots were tied on each harness and everyone who were team members assembled together. We were to climb as a team. We hugged our team and wished other teams the best of luck. Everyone felt a mixture of scared, overwhelmed and devotion towards humongous beauty in the form of the giant snow covered mountains.

Slowly, one by one we started climbing with our teams. Our heart was gripped with euphoria. We looked at each other with a sensation of happiness. Each climber was at a particular distance and we had to maintain that distance while climbing. If one member would fall, it would affect the speed and the balance of everyone.

Our shoes were covered with snow and it was hard to walk on this steep mountain. Snow boots were now showing their importance. Crampons helped to make the grip and move on taking up one step after the other.

Vedant was just ahead me. He kept asking me if I was fine and reassuring me that so was he.

"Do not look back, Vedant. I am fine. You will lose your balance if you keep looking back at me". I had to remind him again and again.

We were all climbing with team spirit looking out for each other. The mountain was huge, but it welcomed us with its hands opened wide. Slowly with one step in front of the other, we kept on climbing with small breaths in between. The beauty of it was so much more than what I had ever imagined. It became so much more, now that Vedant was with me. Vedant was the reason that I stood in this situation today. He was the reason that I started climbing. I felt so happy I could share this moment with him.

Slowly and slowly, the mountain below us grew while the part above us disappeared. We had done it. We had climbed the beautiful beast. We all grabbed the one before us and hugged each other. I hugged Vedant first and then we kept exchanging hugs, congratulating each other.

"We did it. We did it. Yay". Kritika enveloped me in a strong hug.

"Yay". Aryan hugged me tight and then went to hug Kritika.

For the first time, I felt the happiness of being in a team and being successful. The calmness that I felt in when I completed this tough exercise was intoxicating. I loved the peace that I felt inside me. We had gained the confidence now. The climbing down was in the same manner as a team. It felt exhilarating as the cold air mixed with small snowflakes touched and froze our cheeks.

From quite a distance we could see the base camp and felt very happy. Soon, we climbed down and landed. Everyone clapped as we reached the base camp after completing this tough exercise.

'We never know what out there gives us so much happiness while we keep searching for happiness in materialistic things. Technology has driven us away from this beauty. This feeling is nothing less than love'. My mind was running wild yet felt strangely calm.

Thirty-Four

The next day was an emergency training day. We all had assembled for the casualty training.

"So this way you can make a stretcher from the ropes. You get it?" Rajeev sir was teaching us the technique to make a stretcher using rope in case of emergency while climbing.

"Now who is going to volunteer for the casualty person?"

One member from each rope acted as a casualty and other members carried him or her to the base camp on the impromptu stretcher. I was made the casualty person and I lied down on the stretcher.

"Climbing down the glacier with a person in the stretcher is very tough; making grip slowly on the snow and moving forward. So, we are giving you an idea about how to go about it. It may be needed anytime while climbing," Rajeev sir was telling us.

We were now told to trek to a distance of a few kilometres on the hilly sides of the mountains. Carrying a stretcher on the snow trek is a difficult thing. But I, being the casualty person, did not suffer much. Couldn't say much for Aryan and Vedant.

We finally completed this exercise too and soon were back to the base camp.

"Princess, now you can get down". Aryan tilted the stretcher a bit so I could step down from the stretcher as we had reached the base camp.

"I know it was tough. But you could have been the casualty. I told you it should be turn wise," I replied, with a smile. I knew they had to exercise while I had fun lying down on a slow roller coaster.

"No. That is fine. This training was important and I did not want to miss it."

"So, you made me miss it," I made a face and laughed. Aryan laughed too.

"Yes, exactly. Now, you got my point".

Vedant was looking at both of us talking and laughing. I could see him smile from a distance and I smiled back. He was looking at us but his face had no glimpse of jealousy. Possibly things were changing.

Thirty-Five

I do not know how it happened. I never even gave it a thought. But I fell in love with you again when you had that bike accident. I should not have come back to you. I owe that to myself, as well as you Vedant.

I love you. I do and I forever will. You were my first love and I might never be able to love anyone else. But this love has become suffocating to me. I feel imprisoned with you. There is a feeling of loss of freedom, a feeling of losing myself. Love should not feel like a cage. That's what everyone says.

I am a different person when I am with you. That's because I always try to be the best version of what you want me to be. But.., Vedant... I miss being myself. I miss my friends. I miss the feeling of doing things without giving explanations to anyone.

I think I can handle the reality now. You are a different person, Vedant. Whenever you are drunk, you don't remain the person I loved. You say things that hurt me deeply. I tried to ignore them a lot. But what happened last night is something I could not ignore. It made me realize that loving someone and living with someone are two different things. I do not think I can be with you. I know I will always miss you. I might not even find anyone who would love me so dearly; the way you do. But still, I know that I am not prepared to spend the rest of my life with you.

When you came back into my life after our breakup, I should have let you go. It was important to let you go. But I didn't.

Now, however, I can. I am letting you go, Vedant. It means that my love is strong enough to accept the reality and take the step which will be good for both of us. I can never love you truly if I lost myself, my identity. If I lost the girl, the Taara with whom you fell in love with, if I'd not be me, it means we are not in love. I am not that girl anymore. I always have to try to become some updated version for you which is not even the real me... which is suffocating me.

I always wanted to be with you and get married to you. But with time, I have this realization and I want to be away from you to understand my own feelings. Getting away from you is painful but surprisingly, I feel free. Why is it happening? What was wrong in our relationship that makes me feel free when I am away from you? I need to find the answers before taking any big decisions... decisions like getting married to you.

I know if I will stop today, our story will again get complicated. I will be trapped in a cage again while you will be hurt because I won't be able to do whatever you'd want me to. I want it to end on a good note. Maybe this is not the right time for us to be together or maybe there won't be ever a good time for us. Maybe we were not meant to be together. Two people who love each other so much, but cannot exist together.

This time I will not do anything that I am mentally not prepared for because I know it will eventually hurt both of us. I do not want to regret you coming into my life. I am going home for two months. I will come back to give exams. Till then, your exams will be over. I do not want to meet you again. It will help me to stick to my decision. Help me in this as you have always helped me.

Goodbye, Vedant. I am giving the mobile phone to Sarvesh. Take it from him. Please do not try to contact me. If we are meant to be together, the situation will change. Else, we will pass by each other like passing trains that are not meant to go to the same destination.

I love you. I do. But...

Taara

Thirty-Six

"The number you are calling is switched off... again and again. I tried eight hundred twenty six times before the battery ran out. I knew you didn't have it. But I had read the letter when Sarvesh gave it to me. And... and I was crying while reading it. I still have it. It still has the stains of tears on it. Mine, when I was reading it... and yours too. When you were writing it, you cried... You cried..."

Tears were threatening to roll down my eyes again today. When Aryan went away, Vedant joined me and I smiled. I just asked him if he didn't feel jealous of Aryan now. How could he not feel jealous? He told me he still loved me.

"Hmm..."

"That day I realized, Taara. I realized how bad I was for you. I was... I was so drunk that night that I... I overstepped the boundaries. I violated my rights. You loved me... you loved me so much and I knew. I didn't doubt that at all. I was just jealous. I was jealous that I had to share you with others. You know my family never gave me the attention".

I didn't know that. I never noticed it. They gave him so much money, got him admitted to one of the best colleges. I thought they loved him a lot. I never asked him why he didn't talk to his family as frequently as I did. It didn't occur to me at that time.

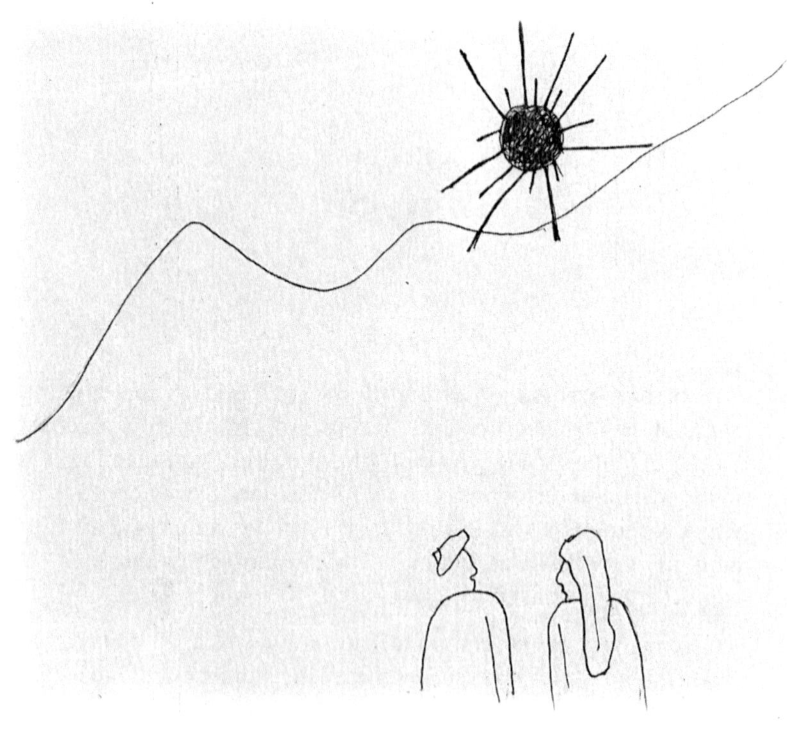

"All I had was you. My parents never had much time for me, ever. They had a lot of money… Yes. But not time. Not even love, I think. They still don't. They didn't want me to come for mountaineering as well. My father's business is his love. My mom loves her causes. I never had many friends … nor any siblings. A lone child who didn't know that people are not toys. They are friends. They were good, you know… the friends in our college. Guy friends. But I wasn't really close to anyone. I didn't really know how to have friends and people that you love. I just had you".

Tears were streaming down my cheeks as the cold air was touching them and becoming cooler on my cheeks. I had no idea how much he never told me. He always knew everything about me… but I didn't. When he didn't tell me, I assumed his life was normal.

"Oh, please don't cry. I don't want you to think it as an excuse for my behaviour. I should not have done it. I am sorry, Taara". A tear glistened on his cheek too as he looked away towards the mountains.

"Taara, I am not telling you all this to influence your decision anyway. You don't have to love me if you don't want to love me. If you… if you love Aryan, that's fine too. I have learnt from my mistakes. I know I can't tie you to me. I lost you once. But now, I feel, at least we can be friends. At least, we can exist together. At least, I will know that I won't suffocate you anymore. That I didn't spoil love for you."

"Vedant…"

"Taara… No. Please. Don't tell me anything now. If you are leaving me again, at least let me live these moments with you. Please don't break this magic. These mountains and you… this was my dream. Please…"

I wanted to tell him that I still loved him. But he didn't want me to tell him now. Maybe he was right. Maybe he will think that I am feeling pity for him after what he just told me. I can't let the future of this relationship again be shadowed by his past. It will be better if we wait till we both are ready finally.

"Let's go back to the tents. It is getting late. We are tired also". I smiled at him. I will tell him soon. I do love him.

Thirty-Seven

The course was coming towards its end. As the days passed, the feelings of not having an excuse to meet Vedant after this course grew more. I was feeling anxious and Vedant too seemed a bit anxious from his glances. But he did not say anything directly and tried to act normal. However, I could sense his feelings.

The competition was growing among the participants. The course was getting tougher and tougher with each passing day and the participants were trying hard to get good scores and grades in the course. It was the basic parameter for the climbers to get into the further advanced courses and mountain expeditions. Aryan and Vedant were competing among the toppers in our course.

"Today we will go for the final expedition of this course. The mountain summit you are going to do today is an actual test of your learning. You will be evaluated individually and the ones who will successfully complete the summit within the time frame are going to get extra marks which later will add up to your overall evaluation of this course. If you are serious about getting into mountaineering in the future and want to do summits on the highest mountain peaks, this one is the trial for you. You will get a basic idea of the challenges that you are going to face there. So, this expedition can be one of the best lessons in this course," Rajeev sir was instructing the participants.

"One thing I would want to tell you all is that, the trek is not easy. If you are stuck somewhere or find it difficult to complete or abandon the trek, you can take your call. We have our coordinators after every few kilometres of distance on the way. You can inform them and they will help you out. When you reach the top, you will meet one of our representatives there too. He will give you the summit completion badge which you will bring along with you to the base camp. For an average climber, the summit should not take more than six hours to reach the top. You all need to be back to base camp by evening. If you are unable to reach the top, even then, you will have to start your journey back to the base camp latest by two in the afternoon. Your lunch is packed and you can carry it with you. In the end, I would advise you to use your physical and mental techniques to complete this summit. Most importantly people, use your heads. It is very important that you have clear and alert minds. I wish you all the best". Rajeev Sir had given all important instructions in one go. It seemed to be a big day and feeling was quite similar to what the movies portray. We felt like soldiers who were carrying the weight of the mission.

I was feeling mixed emotions of motivation and a strange sadness which I was not able to understand. Vedant, I and Aryan walked together. We talked, relaxed and walked as a team.

We had charted out a plan to complete this summit and it seemed perfect. We were supposed to work with each other and it was coming up good.

"We cannot let this opportunity slip from our hands". Aryan was really excited. Probably, he was the only one who was not appearing even slightly nervous. Not more than normal.

"Of course we will do it. Just stick to the plan we have made". I was quite nervous. But I relied on my team. "I am so happy. It feels like I am living my dream. See everything is so beautiful here. The mountains which seemed so beautiful from distance are actually even more beautiful when you get closer to them. But I do feel nervous."

"It's okay if you feel nervous. It's normal. Just stay focused. You will get over the nerves". Vedant was looking deep into my eyes.

We soon had reached a waterfall and we had to cross it. The water level was low and we could cross it slowly holding each other's hands, one by one. Aryan was the first one to reach the other side.

"This map is a bit confusing here. Aryan, have a look, will you?" Vedant handed over the route map to Aryan.

"We need to take the left turn now. See the map. I think we need to go this way". Aryan pointed out to the left direction.

"It seems so. But why are we not seeing any representatives here? There should have been one at such a crucial turn. Don't you think?"

"Yes". I felt a little jolt but that could be my nerves too.

"Hey they said, na. Representatives will be at some distance. May be we will meet them a little further in some more distance". Aryan started walking to the left.

"Aryan, please check again if we are on the right track. We should not lose the path else it will be very difficult to go back."

"Do not worry, yaar. We both are with you. If the path is not right, we will start the journey back. See, as per this map, we had to cross a waterfall on the way and we just crossed one. So, it seems that we are going right". Aryan sounded really confident.

We kept climbing further. As we proceeded further, anxiety grew within me. I felt something was not right. The path was now fully covered with snow. The trek was becoming more and more difficult to walk.

We reached an area which was a bit plain. It seemed so beautiful. The snow covered all around. But all three of us were tensed.

"Vedant, I think we have lost our way. It's already one p.m. and we have not met anyone on the way. The path seems very different from the map too. It's not right".

"Yes, it seems so. But the place looks so beautiful. Isn't it?"

"Yes, but I am worried. We should go back now".

"Let's have our lunch right here and then we can start our journey back. Do not worry".

"Aryan, it seems pretty clear we have lost our way. We should go back now. Have your lunch and we will start journey back to the base camp after that," I said in a loud voice as Aryan stood a bit away from us, looking around the place.

"Okay, Taara. Just give me five minutes. You both stay here. I will just go and take some photographs. See, it's so beautiful here". Aryan moved to his direction.

"Aryan, listen. Do not go away. Stay close to us, okay? We do not know this place".

"Yes.. yes… Do not worry. I will be back in ten minutes". Vedant and I had started to have our lunch. We didn't want to have lunch, but we were pretty hungry.

"I think we lost our way after crossing that waterfall," Vedant said between bites.

"Maybe that is what we think. May be we were on a wrong track from the very beginning. After all, we never actually cleared any of the check points," I said and realized those lines suited well with my relationship with Vedant as well.

Somehow Vedant had felt it too. I could see the change in his face expressions.

"Maybe. But we can always try to come back to right track. What say?" He looked at me hopefully.

"Yes," I said nonchalantly, pretending to not understand the deeper meaning of the line. I wanted to surprise him after the summit.

"When is he going to come back? Aryan behaves very kid like sometimes," I said as we had finished our lunch and were waiting for Aryan to come back.

We looked at the beautiful view around us. We could feel ourselves walking amidst the clouds. At a height of around sixteen thousand feet, you feel like the king of the world. As if the whole world is at your feet and you can see how beautiful everything is.

The wind had started to blow faster and it had started to snow again.

"I think we should go down now. It has started to snow and it will take at least three to four hours to reach the base camp. It's already late," Vedant said, a bit panicked now.

The atmosphere suddenly became tensed. Aryan wasn't back yet and we wanted to start back soon.

"Yes, you are right. But Aryan, he is also not back yet. We should wait for him to come and then we can start the journey to the camp".

"Yes. You are right."

"Aryan! Aryan!" We both tried calling him again and again from different sides, but he did not reply.

"Hey, can you hear something?" Vedant said, coming towards me.

"What? The sound of the wind?"

"Yes. It seems as if some storm is about to come". As Vedant said so, the speed of the wind increased suddenly and it started to snow heavily. Suddenly it felt that all the snow had listened to Vedant and was ready to crash on us together. A very vicious storm was building.

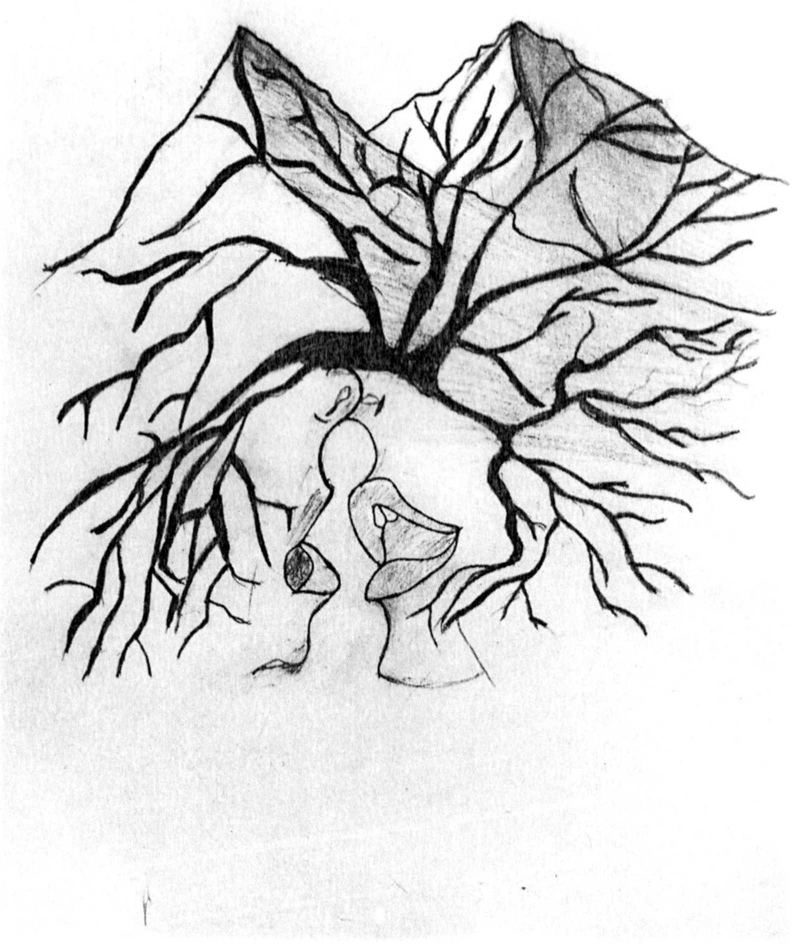

Thirty-Eight

"It seems like the weather is going to get bad. Let's go towards the rocks". Suddenly Vedant pointed towards the rocks at a distance in front of us. They were not very far, but the snow was blinding us and we could not see each other clearly, let alone the rocks.

We both started walking towards the rocks. The strong wind was making the walk more difficult in the snow. After sometime we reached the rocks' area. Vedant looked around and saw a wide gap like a small cave in the rock which was at a small distance from us. He firmly gripped my hand and pulled me indicating to move with him. The snowfall was taking the form of a storm and I could barely see anything around now. Snowflakes were flying with the wind. I could just feel him holding my hand and taking me somewhere and I just followed him. It was just the same way as it used to happen in college days. I always trusted him blindly and this situation was giving me that nostalgic feeling again.

The force of the snow storm was very strong and it didn't feel like it was going to stop any time soon. Moving anywhere right now was not just difficult but very dangerous. There was fresh snow everywhere on the ground as well as snowflakes in the air.

"Hold my hand firmly. Do not leave it". Vedant's loud voice felt like a whisper in all the whistling of the wind but I nodded in agreement.

The sound of the storm and the wind was so profound that we were barely audible and had to talk loudly. We somehow reached the small rock cave.

"Go inside it." Vedant helped me in the cave. I moved inside it and made space for Vedant to slide in. Vedant sat beside me.

"Where is Aryan, yaar?" I was worried.

"I do not know. Nothing is visible. I hope he is safe. For now, we need to stay put in here."

"Aryan..... Aryan....."

Though Vedant called out many times, but he did not get any reply. I too repeatedly called his name and we still couldn't see or hear him. The snow storm was increasing in intensity. We were not prepared at all for something like this to happen.

"What will happen now? This was not expected". I was more worried now.

"I think there was a mistake in studying the weather forecast today. Else, they would have cancelled today's expedition".

"I hope this storm ends soon and Aryan has found some safe place too.". We had no way of finding him now. If he won't get a shelter to step into, he might not make it.

"Yeah. I hope so too, Taara". Vedant ducked his head closer to my shoulder. He was in the outer portion of the cave and was taking all the cold at his back.

It was white everywhere. The snow storm was at its peak. Snow was flying everywhere with great pressure in the direction of the wind. The trees and plants were all covered with snow and were shaking badly. Everything was milky white. We had found a place to hide at the right time else no human being can stand the high force and pressure of such a storm without cover.

"Don't worry, Taara. Everything will be fine". Vedant was looking at my worried face.

"How will we go back to the base camp now? We have lost our way and technically everything will look different outside after the storm. I think we are trapped in here, Vedant".

"We will have to wait for the snow storm to stop. It will stop. After it is a bit controlled, we will start our journey back to the base camp. Hopefully we will find Aryan in between… or maybe he will find us," he tried to assure me.

We sat there for a four full hours. It was getting dark now and the snow storm had taken the form of a blizzard. The snowflakes were getting bigger, bigger than the normal snow and had started to pile up in front of the cave too. Vedant kept on clearing the snow with his hand. We both were freezing now.

"Vedant I think, this storm is not going to stop soon. We are badly trapped in here. We might… might...," I said breaking up inside as I was shivering badly.

"No, we won't. We won't. Wait. I will do something," Vedant said and moved out of the cave.

He broke small branches from the nearby tree and walked back to the cave struggling against the wind. He was shivering very hard now.

"I hope this plan works out."

He took out a knife from his bag. I did not say anything and was just wondering as to what he was going to do. Every muscle I had started to freeze and it felt as if I was destined to die this way. As my body parts were getting colder and colder, they were losing their senses. Blood flow was slowing down and I felt a desperate need to peacefully sleep. I knew I shouldn't, but it felt like my systems were already giving up and I was slowly moving towards my death.

But Vedant kept working; started to cut the branches into smaller pieces and started to peel them into thin wooden layers. He kept doing this for some time and got a bunch of such layers ready which were to easily catch fire as compared to wood itself. He then took out a cigarette lighter from his bag and set the pile on fire. As the fire got a bit stable, he used it to set fire to piled tree branches. I felt a little pain as the blood started rushing in my body soon. It felt like my body was trying to recover what losses it incurred while I felt hypothermic and a warmth began to settle into my limbs soon. It was such a relief. With my body getting back its senses, I was getting back my confidence too.

"Thank you, Vedant".

"I will not let you die, Taara. As long as I am alive, I will keep protecting you," he said looking at me, emotionally.

I bent towards him and hugged him the way I wanted to hug him for all these years. I hugged him for long. We could feel the warmth of each other's body in this freezing cold and I did not want to go away from him again.

"I have missed you so much, Taara. You cannot imagine how difficult it was for me to stay away from you. I have repented my behaviour every moment. Please forgive me," he said with heaviness in his voice. "All these years, whenever I thought about you, I closed my eyes and saw your smiling face. That's how it is imprinted in my mind. I was relieved with the thought that you must be happy somewhere in this world. You know, letting you go was the biggest mistake of my life. In fact, it was the biggest loss of my life. But later on, it brought the satisfaction of setting you free, letting you do what you wanted to do. I do realize that I had been a very possessive boyfriend. That's when I realized how suffocating I had been for you. But I am also sure that no one can love you the way I did and still do. I will not lie to you. I had been in relationships after you went away. I kept hovering from here to there, three to four months in relationships but nothing really worked out. I had realized that I was trying to find you in every girl whom I dated. I always compared them to you, in back of my mind and was never fully into any relationship. None of them worked out. But later it struck my mind, I will never get what I had with you with anyone else in this world. That I cannot love anyone the way I loved you. I am addicted to your kind of love". He paused and slid closer to me. "Please come back to me, Taara. I do not know if you have anyone in your life and I do not want to know too, unless I am too late. Then, I do not want to disturb your life. But, even if there is the slightest chance, please come back to me. I want to love you for the rest of my life".

"Shh," I said releasing from the hug and looking into his eyes lovingly. He held me tight in his strong arms and moved his face closer to mine.

"Shh," he said looking deeply into my eyes and held my face between his hands. He touched my cheeks and then lips gently with his fingers.

The touch had awoken my frozen body and had paralyzed my mind. I did not want to think about right and wrong or the future of this relationship at this moment.

'I love this guy and I will love him forever'. This was all I could think about. I closed my eyes as I could feel his lips on mine. He was kissing me like he had never before. I could feel his love, his passion and the intensity of his feelings for me, as I kissed him back more passionately.

"I love you Taara. I want to spend rest of my life with you. I have already wasted a lot of time. If we survive this, I am not going to let you go away from my life again," he said drifting away a bit but still holding my face in his hands.

I could see the repentance in his eyes. I could feel that his love was true. My soul could connect to the vibes very well.

"We will survive this Vedant. You know why? Because I love you too," I said, assuring him. He smiled and hugged me again.

"We are going to survive this. We are going to live together. Our love story is yet to complete," he said, with all the excitement and love.

"That is why most people get married in winters," I whispered.

"What?" He looked confused, like I had developed AMS suddenly.

"Yes. I mean so that they can hug their partners and not feel cold," I replied, laughing.

He laughed loudly. "Yes. Exactly". He hugged me tightly and we remained in each other's arms without knowing what lay ahead for us.

Thirty-Nine

It had been hours that we were sitting there inside the cave. Vedant and I kept looking at each other. Neither of us was left with strength to talk as our body was freezing. But we kept nudging each other, preventing each other from sleeping.

The cave was too small for two people to fit in properly and Vedant was somehow managing to be inside the cave. I could see his face getting white with cold and his eyelashes got covered with snow as he looked outside. Still the look in his eyes kept assuring me not to lose hope. We hugged each other in some intervals and kept rubbing each other's hands which helped us survive, moment after moment.

Like everything, storm didn't last forever too. Finally, the winds slowed down and snowing almost stopped. We could see we had survived the night. The snow storm had stopped and the visibility had improved outside. We slowly moved out of the cave with little strength left in our body.

"We should look for Aryan".

We both started calling him. We looked around everywhere but could not see him anywhere.

"Taara, we have to start our journey back. We are left with no other option. We cannot wait for Aryan now. We will come with the rescue team to look for him when we reach the base camp," Vedant said with a heavy heart and I nodded in reluctant agreement.

"I hope Aryan is safe. God please help him". I was continuously praying.

Vedant and I started our journey back towards the base camp. There was no more energy left in our bodies. We were walking in the snow with a great difficulty. But this journey had to be completed.

I was finding it difficult to walk, as my legs had started to pain a lot.

"I cannot walk, Vedant. My ankle and leg muscles are paining badly. Maybe because of the ice…"

"Give me your rucksack. I'll carry it. We need to walk, Taara. This is the only option that we have got right now".

We walked slowly through the snow. As we walked, we gained a bit of strength in our limbs as our frozen blood started to flow again in our muscles. Though we had nothing to eat but we knew we cannot give up now after surviving the deadly night. We descended towards the base camp with a lot of halting periods for rest. We both were cold and I was able to walk with great difficulty.

Finally, we reached the point where we had to cross the waterfall again. The time when we had gone ahead, upwards, the water level was very low and we had crossed it by fixing the steps on the big stones in the river. But now, there were no stones to be seen anywhere.

"How will we cross it? Where are the stones on which we crossed it the last time?" I was puzzled.

"Well, it seems to me that the glacier has melted and the water level has risen. The stones may be submerged. We can't depend on stones now. Also the water will be really cold and thinly frozen at places. But we can't step on that, else we will drown under the ice.

"Oh my God..." I said hopelessly. I totally forgot about this. I had no clue as to what we can do now.

"Let me think of something," Vedant said sitting on a stone for resting his back.

He asked me to hold my rucksack and in no time, I could feel his strong arms picking me up, the way he did in the college days and moving ahead.

"What are you doing?", I asked confused.

"I am going to cross the river with you in my arms. The water would be freezing cold and you are hurt too. At least one of us will not get wet."

"But, Vedant, your clothes will get wet and it is not right. We are not in a condition to freeze again. We need our strength so that we can walk to the base camp. You are not going to do this," I said cutting him in between.

"Yes, exactly. We still have to walk to the base camp. So, I cannot let you freeze again. But I am quite strong enough to handle this. Do not worry".

"But...."

"Shhh. Will you keep quiet now or you are finding another excuse for me to kiss you to make you quiet?"

"Huh?"

"I would let you carry me. But come on. That's not possible. So let me carry you. Just so that one of us can retain our strength for the journey ahead. Okay?"

I nodded as he carried me in his arms. The flow of the waterfall was a bit fast. It took him some time to cross it. He had to take every step very carefully so that we don't slip.

Step by step, we reached the other side. It wasn't a very deep waterfall. Vedant put me down on the other side of the waterfall, shivering vehemently. His hands and body were frozen with the cold water drenching his legs.

We rested there as he shivered badly and I hugged him tight. I pressed him to the tree trunk behind and caught him in my arms. I rubbed his hands and foot. I kept hugging him so that he could feel better. Some warmth from my body would help him get his strength back while his teeth were chattering together. We kept sitting there for some time as Vedant's condition was getting worse.

Who was I kidding? The little warmth that I could muster was not keeping me warm. This way Vedant will not make it. I won't be able to carry him. We needed fire. I collected branches from around and kept my hanky around them. Then I lit the hanky on fire with the same lighter of his and put some small branch slices on it. As the fire grew a little stronger, I hugged Vedant again and started rubbing his cold hands.

"Vedant, don't give up. Please. Please. I love you. Please, we will make it".

"Ta... aara. I love you too".

"Get some heat. Vedant, start moving your hands a bit. It will let the blood flow".

As Vedant tried to move a bit, his eyes were drooping with exhaustion. His lips were becoming white and hands were going slightly blue. At this speed, he would lose consciousness very soon.

"Can you hear something, Vedant?" Suddenly I heard some voices.

"Who is thi...s?" We could hear the sound of crushing of dry leaves along with the voice. They were coming towards us.

In no time, we saw four people coming towards us.

"Hey, Taara, Vedant. Thank god you both are safe". Rajeev sir came in view. He saw Vedant sitting near the fire.

"Sir, we were caught in the snow storm. Vedant is wet and very cold. Please help him". As Rajeev sir poured some hot tea into his frozen lips, his colour started getting mildly red. "Aryan is lost, sir. He separated from us. We could not find him. Please send a rescue team to search for him at the top of the peak".

"Do not worry. We have already found him. He is being taken by rescue team to the base camp. I got the message from them sometime back. Actually, we had sent two rescue teams towards both trails. We had sent message to everyone and arranged to bring everyone back as soon as we realised about the snow storm. But we could not find the three of you. I think you went on wrong trek".

"Yes sir"

"Guys, you have setup a nice fire here. Let Vedant dry his clothes and recover a bit. Then, we can move down".

"Tha....ank you..., sir". Vedant looked better after the tea and fire.

I looked up to the sky and silently thanked God. It looked like we were very lucky today. Someone up there was really looking for us.

Forty

As I opened my eyes, I could see Vedant lying on the nearby bed. He was still sleeping but looked better. We both had been given medical treatment and some tranquilizers for relaxing the body muscles. We had been sleeping for quite some time now in the medical tent. The tent was warm because of the room heaters. My leg felt better now.

But the memories of being stuck in cold with no help were still afresh. I remember having nightmare of Vedant's lips going blue and when I heard the voices and I went to look, I didn't find anyone, instead I lost my way. But I knew they will fade in time.

After all this cold, and being frozen for such long time, it felt great to be at a warm place. I felt alive again. All that had happened felt like an adventurous dream that had potential of turning into nightmare. People think that having near death experiences is really fun and heroic, but actually it is very tiring and emotionally draining. It is not at all heroic but really nerve wrecking.

'Did all that actually happen? Of course it did. Thank God it is over'. These are the thoughts that keep running through mind after such experiences. I was still trying to cope with what happened and thank God Vedant was right here in the next cot.

His was coming into my life again and then all these events. It felt like a Bollywood movie which was coming to life… my life. Heroine stuck in storm with an ex, rediscovering love again and struggling to live all at the same time. No matter how funny it sounded, I liked the ending… or the new beginning I should say.

I got up from my bed and went towards him. I held his hand in mine and sat on the ground. I will never leave him again. I love him. The thought made me smile and I bent to kiss him on the lips. As I withdrew, he opened his eyes.

"You are trying to take undue advantage of an innocent unconscious guy, right?", he whispered.

"You are awake".

"I woke up just now. What I was saying is… you can take even more advantage if you want. I am...". I smacked his arm mildly.

"Shut up. Thank God you are alright. How are you feeling now?"

"Much better. Especially now". He got up on his arm.

"I thought we both will die. At one point, I was quite sure of it". Tears slid down my eyes.

"I told you naa, we were meant to be together". He brushed the tears away from my eyes and got onto his feet.

"May be life is just to be lived, not to be understood. When we try to understand life, we forget to live it. So it's better to live life as it comes. At present, it's your presence and our survival of that dreadful night which I thought would have definitely taken our lives. I am so thankful to God that I got you back... twice".

"Twice?"

"Yeah. Once at this course and second with us surviving after crossing that waterfall. Well mostly you. I was scared.

You were freezing and had turned white. Thank God, I got you back again. Now I am not letting you go anywhere"

"Oh no". He mockingly went wide eyed. "Don't behave like a possessive girlfriend?"

I started laughing and he joined in. Then, he stopped laughing and looked deep in my eyes.

"Does your laugh mean that you are my girlfriend now?"

"No. Actually I have already got engaged and I am getting married to someone else soon. I am so sorry, Vedant".

"Not again. You cannot fool me again, Taara". He started laughing again and hugged me. "You did not answer my question?"

"What?"

"Are you my girlfriend now?"

"Yes! Of course, stupid. Now and forever", I replied, kissing his cheek.

"Where did you go, yaar? Thank God you guys are safe. We were so worried about you". Suddenly Kritika, Neeti, Ginni, Sujoy and Aryan entered the tent as we ducked off the embrace and held hands. Lots of group hugs were exchanged.

"We were just talking…". Everyone started laughing suggestively when I remembered the important question. "Where did you go leaving us, Aryan? We were so worried. We thought...we…"

"I am sorry. I just had gone to click some photos like I told you. But then I forgot the way back and got lost. I am sorry. But thank god I found shelter in a broken hut".

"He is lying. He had not gone to take photos. In fact, he had gone to pee," Sujoy said with a laugh.

"Really? But you had to go that far… seriously?", Vedant said, not laughing at the joke.

"Shut up, Sujoy. You could not keep that to yourself... could you? I had gone to pee as well as click some and... the things just messed up?"

"But why were you clicking photos while peeing?" Kritika started teasing him. "That's absurd. Do you have those photos?"

She winked as we all looked at Aryan's face going red. We laughed. There was something in both of their eyes. But who knows?

"Don't tease him."

"Anyhow, now he is an expert in going through emergency situations too. He is a perfect mountaineer now. And he can click photos while peeing". Everyone again laughed as Neeti pulled his leg.

"Yeah, that is true. In fact, all three of us have gone through this special training now which we never asked for". Aryan said laughing too.

"Jokes apart, yaar… it's a good thing that you all came back safe and sound. So, we can celebrate this". And as we were waiting for the cue, we heard the bell to assemble outside and went out.

"Good morning, everybody. As you all know that training is coming to an end. Tomorrow is the last day of your stay here. I hope the journey would have given you an experience for life and... also some clarity in life. Mountains have an everlasting impact in our life. Sometimes we get the answers to the toughest questions which we had been searching everywhere. We get the answers simply by being in the mountains. Sometimes it gives us many other questions to solve. That is why I told you the very first day that mountains can be the best friends but merciless teachers too. Whenever you go near them you learn something or the other," Rajeev sir addressed the assembly.

“So, coming to today’s schedule. You must be wondering what we will be doing today as there is no schedule pasted on the notice board. We have a surprise scheduled for you. We are planning to celebrate the evening with all the participants of this course. Every team should have at least two members participating or a group participation which ever you feel is better. Song, dance mimicry, jokes, whatever is your talent. Take your pick. You have to participate. The program will be at night with the campfire and food.”

“And for now… I would love to see all of you running. At this height of fourteen thousand feet with less oxygen levels, I want to see who completes the run of six kilometres in lesser time. All of you get ready. Aryan, Taara and Vedant. This test is not compulsory for everyone. Those who do not feel fit can stay back”. He said and looked at three of us.

“We will go, sir,” Aryan replied loudly, looking at both of us as we nodded in the affirmative.

“That’s like a true mountaineer. So, all of you can start it now”.

We ran through the road first and the jungles afterwards. It was not a run and seemed more like the trek of my life where I could rest but could not stop. I learnt from the situations and I started running again. I could not stop as long as I was breathing. I was not born to stop. I was born to achieve the heights, the heights that I thought I could never reach. I was taking my steps towards my dream to be at the highest point in the world and see how the world looks from there. The point which is farthest from the earth and closest to the sky. Yes, I will achieve it someday.

The morning bell woke us to have our tea and assemble in the ground in an hour. We had celebrated in the campfire with the songs, dance and Bada Khaana (the celebration dinner). I sang the song ‘Hum Bewafa Hargiz Na The...’ but hummed through most part of it as I forgot the lyrics.

"Taara's song was the best, though it was ninety percent humming," Aryan had teased me after that and everyone including Vedant laughed at this.

Everyone had sad expressions and were depressed to leave the course, friends, the very next day. That parting emotion could be felt in everyone's words including Rajeev sir and Jagdeep sir. They must have to feel that every time the batch left. We all had become a family in the past month. We were all a team now.

We had now assembled in the ground and were being called one by one on the stage for the certificates. Certificates and badges were being given to us by the Chief Guest who was an IAS. She had been part of this course during her training period and was a mountain lover like every one of us who was there for the course. We were given our certificates and badges.

Aryan, Kritika, I and Vedant had got an A plus grade and were happy. Some were sad on not getting desired grades while some had a happy expression of completing the course successfully.

"The course is now over. Empty the tents now and assemble back here in fifteen minutes. We will leave from here in twenty minutes. SUVs are waiting outside for all of you," Rajeev sir announced.

"What?" Everyone was shocked to hear this. We had no idea that we had to empty the place so early and most of us had not even packed the luggage. But everyone knew that here fifteen minutes meant fifteen minutes only.

All of us ran towards our tents. Some ran outside to collect their clothes that were drying out in the sun, while others went to pack their bags. We had to get everything done and be outside in fifteen minutes.

I came out with my rucksack and was ready to leave the place in ten minutes. This course had taught me the value of time. I could see Vedant smiling at me as he had already reached the assembling point. There were a few other participants too.

“You packed so quickly,” Vedant asked.

“I had already done some packing yesterday night,” I told him.

He came near me and held my hand. I looked at him with a puzzled look on my face, not understanding what he was doing.

“Come with me. We still have five minutes”.

“Umm, okay”.

We walked away from the assembly area and stopped at a place where there were just me and Vedant with mountains, and snow surrounding us.

“This is so beautiful. I am going to miss this,” I said, starting the conversation.

“Will you miss me?” His innocent question made me laugh.

“No,” I said, laughing. I said after a pause. “Because I am going to be there with you, stupid”.

I could see his eyes lighting up on hearing this.

“And will you...?” He looked at the mountains and paused.

‘Huh? Is he going to propose marriage to me?’ I thought and looked at him, puzzled.

“Will you go with me to my next expedition… in fact all the expeditions of my life?” He looked into my eyes and held my hand.

"Haha... Yes! Yes, I will, Vedant," I replied, without wasting a second.

We hugged each other and felt the warmth. Holding each other's hands, we looked at the beautiful sunrise. It seemed like the sun of our life was rising afresh, which was warming up our lives. This time we were ready to walk into the bright and cosy morning.

Praise for the author and her works

"*Jeevan Ko Prerit Karti Hai Pustak The Girl Who Saw It All*"

– Dainik Jagran

"*Amazon Par Dhoom Macha Rahi Hai Pustak The Girl Who Saw It All*"

– Khabar Today

"Rooprashi weaves a strong story through her debut novel."

-Ms. Kena Shree, Lifestyle Columnist (web edition)- The Times of India.

"The Girl Who Saw It All is a genuine book with a gripping story."

-Dr. Subodh Kumar Singh, Kashi Ratna & Peat Prize Awardee.

"A must read. The book doesn't give you 'yes' or 'no' answers to questions; but it instead helps us understand the nature of the questions better, so we can answer them for ourselves."

-Lucknow Book Club

"Author Rooprashi has fantastic narration skills and chosen an important topic. This book can be life changing and will make anyone think about the way we live these days."

- The Daily Brunch Team

"*Yuvaon ko prerit karti hai pustak The Girl Who Saw It All*"

-Nav Express.

About The Author

Management Executive, author and blogger, **Rooprashi** is an individual brimming with stories. The author, whose debut novel "The Girl Who Saw It All" made waves across the country, possesses both compassion and composure as well as a capacity for empathy that is clearly reflected in her writing. She writes with an aim to motivate her readers and infuse positivity in society.

Since childhood, she has an artistic bent of mind and was involved in many activities in her school and college. Since, the age of ten, she has been doing stage performances in singing and plays musical instruments including the harmonium, piano, and flute. She is also quite active in sports like table tennis and has participated in "Artificial Wall Climbing" at the national level.

She loves writing motivational and spiritual pieces as well as quotes. For more info on her writing and updates on her latest articles and books, you can visit her website **www. rooprashi.in**

You can also connect with her:

Facebook- **Rooprashi**

Instagram- **@rooprashi**